Mallory's heart clenched like a fist in her chest.

'Thank you,' she said after a moment—which seemed like a better option than *Why don't you kiss me if you think I'm beautiful?* A more sensible option, anyway.

He was her husband. He thought she was beautiful. Mallory sat next to Torr, her pulse booming in the dark, enclosed space of the car. She was burningly aware of his hand on the gearstick, of his massive, reassuring presence. The light from the dashboard illuminated his cheekbone, the edge of his mouth, the line of his jaw, and every time her eyes slid sideways to rest on his profile she felt hollow and slightly sick.

He was her husband. She ought to be able to lean across and put a hand on his thigh. They would share a bed when they went home tonight, but she ought to be able to turn to her husband for more than warmth. She ought to be able to press her lips to his throat, to trail her fingers down his stomach, to kiss her way along his jaw and whisper in his ear.

If he thought she was beautiful, he ought to want her to do that, surely?

Dear Reader

When the sun shines, Scotland can be one of the most beautiful places in the world, and even when it's raining I think it is one of the most romantic too. There's something about the hills and the sea and the smell of the air there that brings up the hairs on the back of my neck. I love it—unlike my heroine, Mallory, who isn't at *all* impressed when she first arrives in the Highlands, but who gradually falls under the spell of the place…and of her own husband.

Although Mallory doesn't share my love of Scotland at the start of the book, we're at one when it comes to dogs. Mine is a West Highland White Terrier called Mungo, now rather elderly, who sleeps under my feet while I'm writing. Mallory's Charlie is a mutt, but no less loveable. He's actually named after a cat, my much-loved tabby, Charlie, who sadly had to be put to sleep just before I began writing this book. I spent so much time thinking about Mallory and how important her dog was to her that I was nearly as fond of the fictional Charlie as of the real one by the time I'd finished!

Jessica

NEWLYWEDS OF CONVENIENCE

BY
JESSICA HART

MILLS & BOON™
Pure reading pleasure

First published in Great Britain 2008
Harlequin Mills & Boon Limited,
Eton House, 18-24 Paradise Road, Richmond, Surrey TW9 1SR

© Jessica Hart 2008

ISBN: 978 0

Set in Times Roman 10½ on 12¾ pt
07-0508-52783

Printed and bound in Great Britain
by Antony Rowe Ltd, Chippenham, Wiltshire

Jessica Hart was born in West Africa, and has suffered from itchy feet ever since, travelling and working around the world in a wide variety of interesting but very lowly jobs, all of which have provided inspiration on which to draw when it comes to the settings and plots of her stories. Now she lives a rather more settled existence in York, where she has been able to pursue her interest in history, although she still yearns sometimes for wider horizons. If you'd like to know more about Jessica, visit her website www.jessicahart.co.uk

For Louise, on her retirement from the CMS, with love

CHAPTER ONE

'THIS year has seen record sales of Valentine's Day cards, while florists report that red roses are still the most popular choice for—'

Mallory reached quickly for the remote control and pointed it at the television to switch off the tail-end of the news. She didn't want to be reminded about Valentine's Day. This time last year Steve had surprised her with a trip to Paris. He had given her a diamond pendant and talked about when they would be married. It had been the happiest day of her life.

Instinctively, she lifted a hand to finger the tiny diamond that nestled at the base of her throat. She wore it still, in spite of everything.

At her feet, Charlie lifted his head from his paws, suddenly alert, and the next moment she heard the sound of a key in the front door.

Her husband was home.

Mallory dropped her hand abruptly.

Charlie was already on his feet, tail wagging. He trotted over to the door of the sitting room, whining and sniffing with anticipation, and would have started scratching at it if Mallory hadn't gone to open it for him. She knew he wouldn't settle until he had welcomed Torr home. He was a dog with a mind of his own.

Mallory had to acknowledge that Charlie wasn't the most beautiful dog in the world—he had a Labrador's soft ears, a collie's intelligent eyes and the bristly coat of a lurcher, but was otherwise a standard, scruffy mongrel—but from the moment she had taken him home from the animal rescue shelter, seven years ago, he had followed her with a slavish adoration.

Perhaps it wasn't surprising that Charlie had been jealous of Steve. He'd been used to being the centre of Mallory's life before Steve came along, and the surly relationship between man and dog had been the only tiny cloud on her horizon in that otherwise golden time.

It was harder to understand the instant attachment he had formed for Torridon McIver, who spent little time with him or his mistress. Charlie was always delighted to see him, though, and didn't seem to mind that he rarely got more than a brusque acknowledgement of his presence in return.

When Mallory opened the door, Torr was standing in the hall, looking through the post she had left on the table for him. He was a tall, forbidding-looking man, with dark hair, stern features and an expression that rarely gave anything away. Raindrops spangled his hair and the shoulders of his overcoat, winking in the overhead light.

When not building a reputation as one of the sharpest and most successful businessmen in the city, Torr went climbing, and it always seemed to Mallory that he carried something of the mountains with him. There was a force about him, something hard and unyielding, that put her in mind of bracing air and desolate peaks. It sat oddly with the expensive suits he wore to the office and with this immaculate Georgian townhouse that he had bought as a sign of his success. They didn't go with the kind of man she sensed him to be.

Any more than she did.

'Down!' Torr ordered Charlie, and when the dog dropped obediently to his belly, tail still wagging ingratiatingly, he bent and gave his head a cursory stroke.

Satisfied, Charlie bounded back to Mallory, and Torr noticed her for the first time as he turned. She was standing in the doorway, and her dark, silky hair fell forward to hide her face as she bent to pat her dog, who pressed his head against her leg, panting gently with excitement. They made an unlikely pair, the dog all bright eyes, scruff and gangly legs, the woman dark and elegantly groomed. In loose silk trousers and a fine-knit top in mushroom colour, she looked stylish and slender to the point of thinness.

'Good dog,' she said affectionately, but when she straightened and her eyes met Torr's, the warmth faded from her face.

'Hello,' she said.

'Hello.'

They faced each other as the familiar constraint crept into the atmosphere. No one looking at them would ever guess that they had been married for five months and that this was Valentine's Day. Torr was hiding no roses behind his back; there was no jewellery secreted in his jacket pocket. He wasn't sweeping her into his arms or telling her he loved her. He wasn't even smiling.

Mallory hugged her arms together and forced her mind away from last year, from Steve, laughing, enveloping her in his golden charm.

'I was just watching the news,' she said after a moment.

Torr shrugged off his overcoat, shaking raindrops on the tiled floor, and hung it up. 'Have you got a minute?'

'Of course,' said Mallory, echoing his stiff, formal tone. They didn't talk very often, but when they did they were always polite.

Charlie bustled into the sitting room behind Torr and flopped down on the rug in front of the fire, satisfied that his two favourite people were where he could keep an eye on them. There was something almost embarrassing in his evident pleasure at getting the two of them together.

It happened rarely enough. By unspoken agreement they had divided up the house into their private domains. This was Mallory's room, in so much as any room felt like hers. The sitting room was beautifully decorated in soft, buttery yellows, the curtains at the large Georgian windows were spectacularly swagged and draped, and the furniture was covered in wonderful fabrics that she had chosen with an unerring eye for patterns that would complement each other without looking as if they had been carefully co-ordinated.

It was a lovely room, and she had been pleased with it when it was done, but it didn't feel like home. Torr had just been a client when she had designed the scheme. Mallory had never dreamt at the time that she would end up living there herself, and in lots of ways she was as much an intruder here as in Torr's large, comfortable study.

Since their disastrous wedding night they had had separate bedrooms, too. Mallory didn't lock her door, but Torr had never set foot inside it. She wondered what he got out of their marriage. She had somewhere to live, and her debts paid in full, but Torr had just ended up sharing his home with a woman he didn't even seem to like very much.

'Sit down,' she suggested, just as she would to a stranger, but Torr stayed looming by the fireplace.

With a mental shrug, Mallory chose an armchair and sat

down herself, and then wished that she hadn't. Torr seemed to tower over her, filling the room with his dark, austere presence. His eyes were the colour of a summer night, a deep, dark blue that should have seemed warm, but they were cool and watchful as they rested on Mallory, and without thinking, she felt for the little diamond at her throat once more. It was impossible to know what he was thinking behind that impenetrable mask.

Not that she was one to talk about masks. What did Torr see when he looked at her? Mallory wondered. He would see the dark, stark eyes, the wide mouth and the fine cheekbones, no doubt, but did he see beyond the mask *she* wore, to the emptiness behind the careful grooming and the careful manners, to the icy numbness that had gripped her ever since Steve had left, to the chill that she couldn't seem to shake, no matter how hard she tried to warm herself?

Torr was blocking most of the heat from the fire, and in spite of the central heating she hugged herself, rubbing her upper arms as the silence stretched uncomfortably.

'How was your day?' she asked at last.

'Successful,' said Torr.

Of course. Torr was always successful. He had built up a multi-million pound construction firm from scratch, acquiring a reputation for toughness—some would say ruthlessness—on the way. As his company expanded, so did Torr's interests. He had a flair for picking up failing companies and turning them into flourishing concerns. There were a lot of people in Ellsborough who owed their jobs to him, even if they had never met him in person. In the city, Torridon McIver was a byword for success.

'How about you?' he asked. 'What have you done today?'

'I've been redoing my CV,' she told him. 'I'm thinking

about applying for a job. I was hoping I could find something to do with interior design again.'

It would mean swallowing her pride and going to some of the consultancies who would once have lobbied to work with her, but Mallory was prepared to do that. She wouldn't let herself think about her own business, destroyed in the fall-out from Steve's scam. She wouldn't remember the reputation she had had, the small but talented team she had built up, how much she had loved her work. When the famous Torr McIver had given her *carte blanche* to design the interior of his new house in the best part of Ellsborough, Mallory Hunter had arrived. Steve had bought a bottle of champagne to celebrate.

No, she didn't want to remember that either. One day she had had everything she'd wished for, the next it had gone. Charlie was all she had left.

Betrayed, bankrupt, Mallory had retreated into a state where Torr's brusque and businesslike approach had been easier to bear than the kindness of friends. He had offered marriage in exchange for the settlement of the crushing debts Steve had left her with, and by then Mallory hadn't cared enough about anything to even hesitate. She had said yes straight away, ignoring the horrified protests of her closest friends.

They had made a deal, and she couldn't go back on it now.

But now, very gradually, Mallory was taking her life back. After months of hiding away, she was starting to see friends again. The effort of talking and laughing and pretending that she was OK sometimes felt like trudging waist-deep through mud, but at least she was trying.

The next step, Mallory had decided, was a job.

Torr was unimpressed. 'You don't need a job,' he said, frowning. 'You're my wife.'

She wasn't much of one. They both knew that. Sticking to their agreement, Mallory turned up to corporate events and was charming to his business associates. She was a perfect hostess when Torr wanted to entertain. She kept the kitchen stocked and the house cleaned. But that was all she did for him.

'I can't sit around all day,' she said. 'I need to do *something*.'

'There'll be plenty for you to do where we're going,' said Torr, and she looked at him blankly.

'Going? Where are we going?'

'Scotland.'

'What?' said Mallory, taken aback.

'The Highlands,' Torr amended helpfully. 'The west coast, to be exact. It's a beautiful area. You'll like it.'

Mallory doubted it very much. She was a city girl through and through. She liked colour and texture, shops and restaurants, art galleries and cinemas. The pictures she had seen of the Highlands showed a wild, inhospitable place that held absolutely no appeal for her.

She was fairly sure Torr knew that too, and when she looked into the navy blue eyes they held a derisive expression that made her certain that he was amusing himself at her expense.

She forced a smile. 'I hadn't realised you were planning a holiday,' she said.

'Oh, this isn't a holiday,' said Torr. 'We're moving. That's what I came in to tell you.'

The polite smile froze on Mallory's lips, and she regarded him uncertainly. 'Moving?'

'I've inherited a property in the Highlands,' he told her, pulling a photograph out of the inside pocket of his jacket and tossing it down onto the glass-topped table next to Mallory. 'That's Kincaillie.'

She picked it up almost gingerly. It showed a crumbling castle squatting on a promontory, almost surrounded by grey, uninviting sea, while in the background a mountain scarred by scree and corries loomed intimidatingly.

Mallory raised her eyes to Torr's. 'Is this a joke?'

'Do I look like I'm joking?'

No, Mallory couldn't say that he did. There was not so much as a suspicion of a smile in his eyes.

Now she came to think of it, she couldn't remember ever seeing Torr smile. He must have smiled sometimes, when he had commissioned her to design this house, or when they had met socially, but if he had she couldn't remember it. Surely he had smiled at their wedding?

But that day was a blank. Only five months ago, but all she remembered about it was the terrible scene on their wedding night.

She looked back at photograph. 'But...this looks like a castle,' she said, still puzzled.

'It is.' To her relief, Torr moved away from the fireplace and sat down on the sofa at right angles to her chair. He lounged easily in one corner, as far away from her as he could get. 'You can only see the medieval part in that view, but there's a later wing behind, so it's more comfortable than it looks.'

'You've inherited a *castle*?' said Mallory in disbelief. She was more than half convinced now that the whole thing was some kind of hoax that Torr was pursuing for his own reasons.

A bit like their marriage, in fact.

'The whole estate,' he said, as if it were the most normal thing in the world to acquire a ruined castle. 'And the title that goes with it, if that interests you. It turns out that I'm the new Laird of Kincaillie,' he went on, an ironic inflexion in his voice, 'and as you're my wife, all evidence to the contrary, that makes you the Lady.'

All evidence to the contrary. Mallory flushed and her eyes slid away from his.

'I didn't realise that you were in line to inherit a castle,' she said uncomfortably.

'Nor did I,' said Torr. 'Oh, I knew that my family had associations with Kincaillie, but I certainly never expected it to be mine. I remember my father took me there when I was sixteen, and my great-uncle was Laird, but he had two sons so it didn't seem likely I would ever inherit. One of them was killed in an accident years ago, and the younger brother had already emigrated to New Zealand by then and didn't want to come back. There's a complicated entail in place which means that Kincaillie can't be sold, so it's been abandoned for the last few years. Apparently he had a heart attack a few months ago, and it took some time for the lawyers to track me down.'

'And you just heard today?'

Torr shook his head. 'I've known for a couple of months. I went up there for a few days as soon as I'd got the letter. I met the solicitors and had a look at Kincaillie again.'

'A couple of *months*?' Charlie lifted his head from his paws as Mallory's voice rose. 'Why didn't you tell me?'

'Frankly, I didn't think you'd be interested.' Torr's expression hardened. 'You haven't shown much interest in my life up to now, have you?'

Mallory coloured. It was true. She had barely known him when they got married, and she had learnt virtually nothing about him in the five months since their wedding.

'If you'd been interested enough to ask where I was going when I went up to Scotland, I'd have told you.'

'I assumed it was a business trip,' she said uncomfortably.

'And I assumed you didn't care one way or the other.'

The truth was that she hadn't. She hadn't cared about anything since Steve had betrayed her and abandoned her and skipped the country, leaving her to deal with the mess he had left behind.

'Why tell me now, then?' she asked.

'Because you'll need to start packing.'

'What for?'

'I told you, we're moving to Kincaillie.'

Mallory drew a breath. 'You're not serious about that, are you?'

'Of course I'm serious.'

'But it's a ruin,' she said, looking down at the photograph again.

'It needs a bit of work, agreed,' Torr replied, 'but you were the one who wanted something to do.'

'A *bit of work*? You only need to look at this picture to see that it's a major restoration project! It'll take for ever.'

'Perhaps,' said Torr, 'but staying in Ellsborough isn't an option. I've sold all my businesses, and I got a good deal on the house, which was confirmed today.'

Mallory was still trying to assimilate the news that he had sold his companies when his last words registered belatedly. 'Which house?' she asked with a sense of foreboding.

'This one, of course.'

'You've sold the house?' she repeated very slowly, an unfamiliar feeling stirring inside her.

Anger.

How strange to feel angry again, she thought with a

detached part of her brain. Strange to feel *anything* after all these months of feeling nothing at all. But that was definitely rage flickering along her veins, warming the iciness inside her.

Torr was watching her face with sardonic amusement. 'I didn't even have to advertise,' he said. 'There were so many buyers who'd expressed an interest if the house ever went on the market that it went straight to auction. Of course, the fact that the interior had been designed by Mallory Hunter just upped the price, as I'm sure you'll be glad to know!'

Mallory surged to her feet, startling Charlie, who sat up and studied her worriedly. He had never seen her like this before, her face bright with fury, her hands clenching and unclenching.

Mallory had never *felt* like this before. The anger was crackling through her. She had once seen a film of a butterfly emerging from its chrysalis, and she had marvelled at the way it slowly spread its crumpled wings. That was how it was for her. The unfamiliar anger was filling her up, warming her, pushing into cracks and crevices until everything that had been weak and crumpled and collapsed about her was smooth and whole again, until she was Mallory Hunter, grown woman of thirty-two and successful interior designer, instead of the broken, beaten shell Steve had left behind.

'Without even *discussing* it with me?' she demanded of Torr, who regarded her with a kind of speculative interest, noting how the dark brown eyes, dull for so long, were suddenly flashing.

'Why should I?'

'I'm your wife!'

'Only when it suits you,' he said brutally. 'Like when you needed me to pay off all your debts, for instance.'

Mallory flushed, but stood her ground. 'We had an agreement,' she reminded him. 'You said you needed a hostess, someone to help you with entertaining who wouldn't make any emotional demands on you. I needed somewhere to live where I could have Charlie with me, and, yes, you would settle my debts. But that was the *deal,*' she said fiercely. 'The house was part of that, and now you're telling me that you've sold it out from under me without even mentioning the possibility!'

'I'm providing another home,' said Torr indifferently. 'And one Charlie will like a lot more than this one.'

Hugging her arms together against the sick, panicky feeling, Mallory turned away. The anger was already fading, leaving her feeling trapped and suffocated. There had to be some way out of this. All she had to do was keep calm.

She drew a deep breath. 'Look, can we talk about this? I know how much I owe you, and that I haven't been very... forthcoming,' she said, and moistened her lips. 'You're right, I haven't made much of an effort to make our marriage work so far, but I will,' she promised. 'I've realised that I have to find a way of moving on from Steve.'

Torr's expression was far from encouraging, but Mallory gritted her teeth and ploughed on. 'We got off to a bad start,' she tried again.

'That's one way of putting it,' he said, with a short, unamused laugh.

There was an unpleasant silence, and for Mallory it was as if they were both back in that expensive, awful hotel room, at the moment when she had realised, much, much too late, what a terrible mistake she had made.

'Don't do it,' her friend Louise had said, appalled. 'You can't marry a man you don't love. You'll be miserable.'

But Mallory hadn't listened. She'd already been miserable, and nothing could change that. Torr knew that she didn't love him, she had reasoned, and it didn't bother him. He had had enough fake emotion from his ex-wife, he had told her.

'I don't expect you to pretend that you're in love me,' he had said when he'd asked her to marry him. 'I know how you feel about Steve.'

Theirs would be a purely practical arrangement, they had agreed. There would be no pretence, no sentimental rubbish about love, and at the time it had made sense. More than that, marriage to Torr had seemed to Mallory her only option at the time.

She had thought that she would be able to go through with it. She had even anticipated how difficult the wedding night would be, but had told herself that it would be all right. Arranged marriages were common in some parts of the world, and had been here in the past. If other women could deal with it, so could she.

She made sure that she kept taking the Pill, though. A loveless relationship might be the only option for her, but there was no way she would make a child part of it. Mallory had thought she was prepared.

But when Torr had reached for her that night she had been unable to prevent a flinch at his touch, and she had put her hands over her face.

'I'm sorry,' she had whispered. 'I *can't*. I just can't. I can't bear anyone but Steve to touch me.'

Mallory didn't blame Torr for being angry. His cold contempt had lashed at her, and the memory of what he had said still stung, but it was no more than she thought she deserved.

'You can divorce me,' she had offered at last, but Torr wouldn't hear of it.

'And admit that I'm a failure to the whole of Ellsborough?'

he had snarled. 'I don't think so. No. Do what you like when you're alone, Mallory. If you want to waste your life pining for that lying, cheating, cheap thief Steve Brewer, be my guest, but as far as everyone else is concerned our marriage going to be a *success,*' he'd finished, practically spitting out the word.

So, between Torr's refusal to admit that he could be associated with anything less than total success, and the unspoken reminder of just how much money he had paid out on her behalf, the hollow sham of their marriage had continued. As long as Mallory kept up appearances as the perfect corporate wife, Torr left her alone.

Mallory should have been grateful, but it was a bleak and bitter way to live, and she had been wondering recently how she could try and put things between them on better footing somehow. But Torr showed no interest in meeting her halfway, and in the face of his continued icy withdrawal, her fragile confidence had faltered.

Now she would have to try again.

'I feel like a train that's been derailed,' she tried to explain. 'Ever since Steve left, it's as if I've been stuck on my side, wheels spinning but going nowhere. I haven't been able to do anything but go through the motions of getting through every day. But I know it's time I got myself back on track somehow.'

Torr's expression was as unresponsive as ever, and desperation curdled in her stomach as she saw her last support being cut out from beneath her. 'That's why I've started applying for jobs,' she said, hating the way her voice quavered. 'I need to work again, to start seeing my friends again. We could make a go of our marriage if we stayed here,' she promised, but Torr was unimpressed.

'No reason why we shouldn't make a go of it in Scotland,' he said.

Mallory threw pride to the winds. She couldn't face being wrenched away from everything familiar just when she needed it most and dumped in the wilds of Scotland. 'If you want me to beg, I will,' she said desperately, 'but please don't make me go. This is my home.'

'You'll have a new home,' said Torr.

'A ruin?' Mallory laughed wildly. 'Oh, yes, I can see myself settling there!'

Torr only shrugged. 'Home is what you make it.'

Mallory felt very cold. She stood right in front of the fire, clutching her arms together, but she couldn't get warm. As her momentary hysteria faded, she raised her head and looked at her husband with stark brown eyes.

'You're doing this to punish me, aren't you?'

Something flickered in his expression. 'Why would I want to punish you, Mallory?'

'You know why.'

'What? You think I've sold up and bought a ruined castle just because my wife can't stand me touching her?' he said roughly. 'You don't mean that much to me, Mallory.'

She flinched at his tone. 'Then why go to all the trouble of moving?' she asked.

'Because I want to,' said Torr. 'Kincaillie's mine.' There was a note in his voice that she had never heard before, something warm and intense that made her look at him sharply.

'I'm not making you do anything,' he told her. 'If you want to stay here in Ellsborough, stay. It's your choice. But this house is sold, and I've agreed a completion date in a month's time, so you'll have to find somewhere else to live.'

And two hundred and fifty thousand pounds. Torr didn't

actually say it, but the words seemed to hang in the air between them.

Where could she find that kind of money? It didn't occur to Mallory that the debts had been paid and that she could walk away from the marriage now that the financial fall-out had been settled. The only difference now was that she owed Torr instead of numerous other angry creditors.

Wearily, Mallory dragged the hair back from her pale face. It was easy to blame Steve, but she had to take responsibility too. She was the one who had persuaded Torr to invest in Steve's plan to convert some of the old warehouses down by the river.

She had been so thrilled by Steve's designs. For her, it had been the start of a wonderful career, working together to restore and convert interesting buildings. They had planned it all—how he would do the building, she would do the interior design. Together, they would be the perfect team. Without a moment's hesitation she had remortgaged her house and her company, and committed herself to a proper business partnership with Steve. Steve had suggested it would be a good idea to keep everything legal.

It had meant that when he absconded with all the money they had raised from investors in the warehouse project Mallory had been left liable for everything.

Torr hadn't been one of those demanding his investment back. 'More fool me,' he'd told Mallory. 'I should have checked more carefully.' Other creditors had been less understanding, until her marriage to Torr had meant that all debts could be settled in full.

A quarter of a million pounds. It might not seem much to Torr, but to Mallory it was an awful lot of money and she couldn't imagine ever being able to repay it all.

She bit her lip. It wasn't just the money keeping her tied to Torr. Her house had been repossessed, and with no job and no money to pay rent she had been desperate for somewhere to live. For a while she'd stayed on friends' floors, but she hadn't been able to do that for ever. Her sister had offered to have her, but she lived in an apartment block where no pets were allowed.

'Why not take Charlie back to the shelter?' she had suggested gently to Mallory. 'They'll find him another good home.'

But Mallory hadn't been able to do that to Charlie, or to herself. His unwavering trust and affection were all that got her from day to day.

That had left marriage to Torr.

It still left marriage to Torr.

Torr had been watching her face. 'It's time you decided what you want, Mallory,' he said abrasively. 'What you want and what you're prepared to do for it. If you don't want to come to Kincaillie, fine. Go and stay with your sister, get yourself a job, and start paying back the money your scumbag of a partner stole.'

'You know I can't take Charlie to my sister's.'

'I'll take him to Kincaillie with me, in that case.'

Mallory whitened. 'You're not taking Charlie from me! That's blackmail!'

'It's not blackmail,' said Torr with an impatient gesture. 'It's telling it like it is. The choice is yours. Stay here on your own, or keep Charlie and come to Kincaillie with me. We can make a fresh start,' he said. 'God knows, we both need it.'

There was no way she would let Charlie go without her. It wasn't much of a fresh start, Mallory reflected. She was trapped, and Torr knew it.

'All right,' she said heavily, 'I'll come.'

CHAPTER TWO

THE car had been bumping slowly along a rough and pot-holed track for what seemed like hours. Angry gusts of wind buffeted the vehicle, and the windscreen wipers swept frantically backwards and forwards against the sleeting rain that blurred the powerful beam of the headlights. They had been driving for over eleven hours, the last few through utter darkness, unbroken by lights or any sign of human habitation, and Mallory was so tired that it took her some time to register that they had actually stopped at last.

Peering through the horizontal rain, Mallory could just make out a massive stone doorway.

The wind screamed round them, shaking the car like a terrier with a rat, and Torr had to raise his voice above the noise.

'Welcome to Kincaillie,' he said.

Mallory didn't answer. Her hand crept to the diamond around her neck, and she squeezed her eyes shut, pretending that this was just a nightmare, and that when she opened them she would find herself lying next to Steve, warm and loved and happy, with the sun pouring golden over the bed.

But when she forced herself to open her eyes again, it was to the sickening realisation that this was all too real. The rain was still splattering against the windscreen; the wind was still raging and howling. The blackness and emptiness were still pressing frighteningly around them, the way they had since they'd left the nearest village behind some twenty miles before, and instead of Steve there was only Torr, who had been silent and grim-faced the whole way.

At her feet, Charlie stirred and whimpered. The car was packed so tightly that he had had to spend the entire journey in the cramped seat well. Mallory rested her hand on his bristly head, unsure whether she was giving reassurance or drawing it from the warm comfort of his presence.

Torr turned off the engine and reached into the back for a torch. 'I'll show you inside first, and then we'll unpack.'

Mallory couldn't move. Pinned into her seat by a combination of exhaustion and fear, she clutched at her diamond once more. But it was as if the sunny, happy world she had lived in with Steve had vanished completely, and now there was only darkness and cold and loneliness.

And Torr.

Her husband. A stranger.

He switched off the headlights, plunging them into pitch-darkness, and Mallory was unable to prevent a gasp of fright before he clicked on the torch.

'Come on,' he said, and then, when Mallory still didn't move, 'Unless you want to sit here all night?'

No, she didn't want that, but she didn't want to get out into the wild night either. Mallory hesitated, but when Torr opened his door she reached for the handle. There was no way she was staying here alone. If she could have a hot bath, a stiff drink and a comfortable bed to fall into and sleep for a week, she could start putting this hellish journey behind her. It was clear that she wasn't going to get any of those in the car.

Which meant she would have to get out too.

The wind was so strong that she had to force open the door until it was wide enough to get out, and then stand braced against it while Charlie leapt down, delighted to stretch his legs at last. Oblivious to the cold and wet, he ran around in circles, sniffing vigorously.

Mallory wished she could ignore the conditions that easily. The wind tore at her hair and the sleet stung her eyes and cheeks as she toiled after Torr, then stood shivering and clutching her jacket around her while he reached for the door.

'This is the point where you realise that you've lost your key and we have to drive all the way home,' she shouted over noise of the wind, not sure if she were joking or wishing that it was true.

Joking, she decided. After eleven hours, there was no way she was getting back into that car for a while, even if it did mean heading back to civilisation.

Illuminated by the headlights, Torr turned the great handle and shouldered open the door with a creak that would have won an Oscar for best sound effect in a horror movie.

'This *is* home,' he pointed out sardonically. 'And there aren't any keys.'

As soon as she stepped inside, Mallory could see why security wasn't a major issue. Although 'inside' was a generous description, she realised with dismay as Torr played the torch around a cavernous hall. It wasn't only the creaks that belonged in a film.

The whole place could have been a set for a *House of Horror.* Weeds were growing through the flagstones, and there didn't appear to be a roof, judging by the icy rain that continued to drip down her neck. They were sheltered from the worst of the wind, but that was about as inside as it got. Who needed a key, anyway, when there was nothing to steal?

Aghast, Mallory followed the powerful beam of the torch as it touched on gaping rafters, a massive fireplace filled with soot and rubble, a magnificent but rotting staircase, birds' nests tucked into strange nooks and crannies, piles of unidentifiable debris and—yes!—that really was a coat of armour, propped in one corner and liberally festooned with cobwebs. All that was needed was for a corpse to pop open the visor, or for a swarm of bats to swoop down on them, and the scene would be complete.

Mallory had the nasty feeling that she was teetering on the edge of hysteria. She was so tired and so cold and so miserable, and this awful place was so much worse than she had even imagined, that she didn't know whether she was going to burst into tears or manic laughter.

But she hadn't cried at all since Steve had left, and now was not the time to start.

'This is cosy,' she said as she huddled into her jacket and the wind and rain swirled down through the hole in the roof.

'I'm glad you like it.' Rather to her surprise, Mallory detected an undercurrent of amusement in Torr's voice. It was too dark to read his expression, but he sounded as if he appreciated her sarcasm. But then, she thought bitterly, he might just have been enjoying how appalled she was by the conditions.

'The kitchen is in rather better condition,' he promised.

Mallory sighed. 'I can't wait.'

'It's down here.' Torr set off towards a doorway in the far corner of the hall, and Mallory whistled nervously for Charlie. This was no time to get separated.

Charlie came bounding in to join them, and followed, happily sniffing, as Torr led the way down a dank passageway with a low, vaulted ceiling and all sorts of turns and unexpected steps that made Mallory stumble, although Torr never did.

He strode on for what seemed like miles, bending his head occasionally when the ceiling dipped but otherwise apparently oblivious to the potential horrors that might lurk around every twist in the passage.

Mallory's earlier bravado had disappeared the moment Torr headed into the passageway, and her heart was thumping. Charlie was unperturbed by the darkness or fear of the unknown, and she wished passionately that she had his lack of imagination. As it was, she had to hurry to keep up with Torr, and when he paused briefly at a fork in the passageway, she threw pride to the winds and took hold of his jacket.

Torr glanced down at her. 'Frightened?'

'Of course I'm frightened!' she snapped. 'I'm stuck in a haunted castle in the pitch-dark, miles from anywhere, and the way my luck is going at the moment I'm heading straight for the dungeons!'

'No, the dungeons are the other way,' said Torr, but to Mallory's secret relief he took her hand. 'We're almost there,' he told her. 'It just seems further in the dark when you don't know where you're going.'

His clasp was warm and firm and extraordinarily reassuring. Mallory immediately felt better, and tried not to clutch at him, although there was no way she was letting his hand go. 'There aren't really dungeons, are there?' she said nervously.

'I wouldn't be surprised. This is a medieval castle, after all.'

'Great. They're probably full of skeletons, too.' Mallory shuddered. 'This whole place is probably choc-a-bloc with ghosts!'

Torr tsked. 'There's no such thing as ghosts.'

'That's what they always say at the beginning of a horror movie when they start exploring a ruined castle in the middle of nowhere!'

'I always thought you were a sensible woman,' said Torr disapprovingly. 'Certainly not the kind to believe in that kind of nonsense.'

'I didn't used to be—but that was before I started hearing the sound of chains being rattled in the darkness!'

'You won't hear ghosts from the dungeons here, Mallory. This wing is modern.'

She stared at him. '*Modern*? In which csentury?'

'The nineteenth,' he conceded. 'Long past the age of dungeons, anyway.'

'Pity it wasn't in the age of electricity!'

'Electricity we have,' Torr announced. 'If you just give me a minute… Ah, here we are! Hold this a moment,' he said, handing Mallory the torch.

Pushing open a door, he felt round for a switch inside and a couple of naked light bulbs wavered into life. The light they offered was pretty feeble, but after the pitch-blackness of the passage, Mallory blinked as if dazzled by searchlights.

'This is the kitchen,' he said.

She looked around the huge, stone-flagged room. At least this one had a ceiling that appeared to be intact, and at first glance there were no weeds or suits of armour, but otherwise it was dank and dirty and depressing.

'Is that better?' Torr asked her.

A little puzzled by his tone, Mallory glanced at him, only to see that he was looking down to where she was still clutching his hand. She dropped it as if scalded, appalled to feel a faint blush stealing up her cheeks.

'I thought you said the dungeons were the other way,' she said to cover her confusion, and Torr clicked his tongue.

'You've got everything you need,' he said, waving in the direction of an array of old-fashioned ranges. 'Somewhere to cook. A sink. Even a fridge and freezer,' he added, pointing at a grimy model of the kind she had once seen in a museum of everyday living. 'All the mod cons.'

Mallory sighed. 'I'll have to get used to the fact that when you use the word "modern" you're talking about a hundred and fifty years ago! Personally, I've never seen any cons *less* mod!'

'Oh, come on. It's not that bad. You've got electricity—and masses of storage space,' Torr added, with a comprehensive sweep of his arm.

She couldn't argue with that. There were not one but two huge pine dressers, an enormous kitchen table, worn from years of use, and old-fashioned cupboards running almost the length of the long room, and that was before she even started opening various doors to find larders and the like.

'Shame that we haven't got anything to store, then, isn't it?' she said to him a little tartly.

Almost everything had gone into storage, and they had only brought with them what could fit in the car and its tarpaulin-covered trailer. 'We won't need much to begin with,' Torr had said. 'Just bring the essentials.'

The 'essentials' would fill one cupboard if they were lucky.

'Better to have too much space than too little,' he pointed out.

There was certainly space. The ground floor of Mallory's house in Ellsborough would have fitted easily into the room. At one end there was an enormous fireplace, with a couple of cracked and battered leather armchairs in front of it which made a separate living area.

'My great-uncle pretty much lived in this room on his own for the last few years, before his son moved him to a nursing home,' Torr said when Mallory commented on it. 'He couldn't afford to keep up the castle, but he refused to leave until he was in his nineties and they couldn't find anyone prepared to come in and care for him here.'

'I can't imagine why,' Mallory murmured, with an ironic glance around the kitchen.

'They put a bathroom in one of the old sculleries for him.' Torr opened a couple of doors. 'Yes, here it is.'

He stood back to let Mallory peer in. There was a rudimentary bath, half filled with droppings, dust and cobwebs, a grimy sink and an absolutely disgusting lavatory.

So much for her fantasy of a hot bath before falling into bed.

Charlie, who had been sniffing interestedly round the kitchen, put his paws on the loo seat and began slurping noisily at the water, obviously feeling right at home.

Look on the bright side, Mallory told herself. It can't get any worse than this.

'Where did your great-uncle sleep?' she asked wearily.

'I'll show you.'

There was a short passage leading out of the kitchen, and Torr threw open another door. 'I think this used to be a sitting room for the upper servants,' he told Mallory, who had finally managed to drag Charlie out of the bathroom. 'But, as you can see, it makes a perfectly adequate bedroom.'

That was a matter of opinion, thought Mallory.

'It's got a ceiling, I'll give it that,' she conceded.

'And a bed,' Torr pointed out, indicating a rusty iron bedstead complete with lumpy mattress. 'And a wardrobe and a chest of drawers. What more do you want?'

Mallory thought of her comfortable bedroom back in Ellsborough, with its dressing table and the pretty little sofa. The curtains were swagged and trimmed, the colour and pattern of the fabric picking up the tones in the bedspread and upholstery perfectly so that the whole effect was one of freshness and tranquillity.

She sighed. 'I wouldn't know where to start,' she said.

Still, she was so tired that she thought she would sleep anywhere that night—until a thought occurred to her.

'Where are you sleeping?' she asked cautiously.

'Right here,' said Torr. 'With you. There's no need to look like that,' he added roughly. 'I'm well aware of how you feel. You made it clear enough on our wedding night, and frankly I've no desire to repeat the experience myself. It was like being in bed with a marble statue, which isn't my idea of a turn-on,' he added with a caustic look. 'I won't have any problem keeping my hands off you.'

Mallory stiffened at the asperity in his voice and lifted her chin, the appalling conditions momentarily forgotten. 'If you feel like that, I'm surprised you want to share a bed with me,' she said.

'I don't particularly,' Torr told her, 'but I don't have much choice. These are the only habitable rooms at the moment, and one bed is all we've got. It's too damp and cold to sleep on the floor, so we might as well be practical about it. If nothing else, we can keep each other warm,' he went on as he led the way back to the kitchen.

'Why didn't you tell me about all this before we came?' demanded Mallory, hating the fact that she always ended up trotting after him, but lacking the courage to be left on her own. 'You must have known that we would end up sharing a bed.'

'Would it have made a difference?'

She thought about how few options she had if she wanted to keep Charlie. 'Probably not,' she admitted grudgingly, 'but at least I would have been prepared.'

'I can't see that it would have helped,' said Torr indifferently as he retrieved the torch and clicked it back on. 'You weren't going to like anything about Kincaillie, so there was no point in giving you something else to feel miserable about. You were just going to have to accept it anyway.'

'Because I can hardly walk out if I don't like it, can I?' said Mallory bitterly. She glanced up and caught a glimpse of Torr's answering smile.

'It would be a very long walk,' he agreed.

Unpacking the car seemed to take a very long time. The wind shrieked and clutched at them as they toiled backwards and forwards, and by the time they had finished Mallory's hands were numb with cold and the icy rain had plastered her hair to her head. She was wearing the waterproof jacket that she used when she walked Charlie, but the hood was worse than useless in this wind, and she had given up trying to keep it on her head. As a result the sleet had found its way around her neck and seeped horribly down her back. It wasn't too bad as long as she kept moving, but the moment she stopped, she shivered with the clammy cold.

Torr had decreed that they could leave it until morning to unpack the trailer, but they still ended up with a pile of boxes in the middle of the kitchen floor. Mallory was ready to drop with exhaustion, but Charlie still had to be fed. It was long past his supper time, and he had been patiently accompanying them in and out to car in the hope that his bowl would materialise.

Peeling off her jacket with a grimace, she hung it over the

back of a chair and began looking through boxes for the dog food. Torr had brought a portable gas ring with him, and connected it to the canister. His movements were quick and competent, and Mallory found herself watching him from under her lashes as she spooned food into Charlie's bowl. She had never really noticed that about him before now. She had seen him as the brusque, successful businessman that he was, but she had never thought of him *doing* anything apart from making money. He seemed to know exactly what he was doing.

She put the bowl down on the floor and Charlie waited, quivering with anticipation, for her signal that he could eat. Mallory smiled at his expression. 'OK,' she said, and the dog leapt for the bowl, wolfing down his meal in matter of seconds and then deriving a lot of enjoyment from pushing the bowl around as he licked it clean. The stainless steel rang on the stone floor, and Mallory made a mental note to find his plastic mat for next time.

Hunger satisfied, Charlie slurped water noisily, and then threw himself down on the tattered rug in front of the fireplace and rested his head on his paws with a sigh of contentment.

Torr glanced at him. 'Must be a nice being a dog sometimes,' he commented dryly, setting a kettle on the gas ring and lighting the flame.

'I know. A bowl of dog food and somewhere to stretch out and he's perfectly happy,' said Mallory, swaying with tiredness. 'I'll pass on the dog food, but I wouldn't mind somewhere to lie down myself. Did you bring in the bedding?'

'I put it in the bedroom.'

'I'll make the bed, then.'

She might as well face up to it, Mallory had decided. Sharing a bed was obviously part of Torr's punishment, and she wasn't going to give him the satisfaction of making any more fuss about it. No doubt he was expecting her to insist on sleeping on her own somewhere, but she was so tired she had to lie down, and it looked as if the bed was her only option. It would take more than Torr to stop her sleeping tonight, in any case.

The little bedroom was freezing, and Mallory shivered as she covered the lumpy mattress with a blanket and then made the bed, layering it up with a duvet and three more blankets on top. Even in the meagre light of the single naked bulb it looked positively inviting.

To Charlie's delight, Torr had laid a small fire, and the flames were just starting to take hold when she went back into the kitchen. The fire was dwarfed by the enormous fireplace, but it was surprising how welcoming it looked, and at least it gave the illusion of warmth, even if not the reality.

'I've made some tea,' said Torr. He nodded at the sagging armchairs in front of the fire. 'Sit down.'

He had thrown a travelling rug over the chair, presumably in lieu of a good clean, but Mallory was beyond caring. She dropped gratefully into one of the chairs and took the mug of steaming tea that Torr handed her with a murmur of thanks, cradling her hands around it for warmth.

'I'll get the range going in the morning,' said Torr, bringing his own mug over to sit in the other chair. 'That'll warm the place up.'

'Warm? What's warm?' Mallory huddled in her chair and watched disbelievingly as Charlie heaved a sigh of content-ment and rolled onto his side, stretching out his paws towards the fire as if he were perfectly comfortable. 'I can't even remember what it feels like!'

Staring into the flames, she thought longingly of her little centrally heated house, which had been repossessed along with everything else when Steve disappeared. All she had been left with was humiliation and a huge debt.

And a husband who despised her.

She sighed.

'You'll like it better in daylight,' said Torr, almost roughly.

'I hope you're right,' she said, reflecting that it could hardly seem worse. She glanced at him. 'What is there to like?'

'The hills, the sea, the peace,' he said promptly. 'The smell of the air. The sound of the birds. The space. There are no beeping phones, no e-mail, no deadlines, no hassle.'

Mallory looked at him in surprise, momentarily diverted from her shivering. 'I thought you thrived on all that,' she said. 'Don't you need the adrenalin rush of wheeling and dealing?'

'I prefer the adrenalin rush I get from a difficult climb,' said Torr. 'That's not to say I haven't got a kick out of building up my businesses, but my original plan was just to earn enough to buy a place in the country. Not as big as this, of course, but a farm, or somewhere I could live off the land. The trouble with success, though, is that it brings along responsibilities,' he went on. 'Once you start to employ lots of people, you realise they're depending on you for their livelihoods, and it becomes harder and harder to contemplate selling up.'

Mallory's expression must have been more sceptical than she'd intended, because he stopped then. 'That makes it sound as if I was just making money for the sake of my employees, which of course wasn't the case,' he acknowledged. 'And I *did* get a buzz out of pushing through a difficult deal, or winning a big contract. It's easy to get sucked into feeling that if you can just do one more deal, make one more million, the time will be right to give it up. But then there's another deal, another million to be made... Who knows how long I'd have gone on if the letter telling me that Kincaillie was mine hadn't arrived?'

Torr leant forward to add another log to the fire, and the flickering light threw his stern features into relief. Watching him over the rim of her mug, Mallory reflected that she had learnt more about him in the last minute or so than she had in the five months of their marriage. He hadn't really told her anything about himself before.

And she had never asked.

She wriggled her shoulders, as if to dislodge the uncomfortable thought.

'That letter stopped me in my tracks,' Torr went on, unaware of her mental interruption. 'It made me realise that I was a long way down a road I had never intended to take for more than a little way, and I had to make a choice. I could carry on making money, or I could give it all up and come back to Kincaillie.'

'Come *back?* I thought you only came here once?'

'I did, but Kincaillie is a big part of our family mythology. My father used to talk about it a lot, and he heard about it from *his* father, who grew up here. He was a younger son, so he left to make his own way in the world, but he never forgot Kincaillie, and my father was brought up on stories of the place.'

Torr stirred a log with his foot. 'I never expected to own Kincaillie, but I was always aware of a connection. It's a special place. I felt it when my father brought me here as a kid, and then again when I came to see it a month ago. I still can't really believe that it belongs to me,' he confessed. He looked around him. 'It's like a fantasy coming true just when you least expect it. I can't believe I'm sitting here at last and it's all mine.'

Mallory followed his gaze around the grim kitchen, comparing it with the stunning Georgian townhouse they had left behind. That house had been the last word in style and elegance, its spectacular kitchen bristling with state-of-the-art technology and cutting-edge design. Torr had given all that up for *this?*

'How does it feel?' she asked him, and his eyes came back to hers.

'It feels like coming home,' he said.

Mallory had the strangest feeling that all the air had been suddenly sucked out of the room. Worse, her eyes seemed to have snagged on his, and she couldn't look away from his gaze. 'I can't say it's my fantasy,' she managed a little unsteadily after a moment, and something closed in his face.

'There's no need to tell me that,' he said curtly.

'I wouldn't have thought you were a man who went in for dreams and fantasies much yourself.' Mallory had been hoping to lighten the atmosphere, but instead her words came out almost accusingly.

Torr's eyes flickered, and he turned back to look at the fire. 'You'd be surprised,' he said.

It turned out that there was a door which led directly into a kitchen garden, and Mallory was hugely relieved to discover that she didn't need to negotiate that creepy passage on her own in the dark to take Charlie out.

'I'll take him if you like,' Torr offered brusquely as he got to his feet and collected their empty mugs. 'You get ready for bed.'

I won't have any problem keeping my hands off you. Mallory could still hear the contempt in his voice, see the dislike in the navy blue eyes. She hadn't expected him to be thoughtful enough to give her time to get ready by herself, and she hurried gratefully to take advantage of his offer.

Relinquishing her own fantasy of a deep, hot bath, Mallory did her teeth in a sink in the scullery. It was dank and grimy, but not as bad as that horrible bathroom, and she was too cold and too tired to start cleaning now.

Her teeth chattered uncontrollably as she headed into the bedroom. She might have decided not to make a fuss about the situation, but that didn't mean that she was ready to casually undress in front of Torr.

Although it was more a case of putting clothes on than taking them off, Mallory reflected wryly, digging through her case in search of yoga pants and a sweatshirt. She hadn't expected to be sharing a bed, and they were the best she could do. It was just as well she hadn't had any hopes of seduction. This was no place for sexy nightwear, even if she hadn't thrown all hers away when Steve had abandoned her.

As quickly as she could, Mallory pulled off the trousers and jumper she had travelled in and wriggled out of her underwear, sucking in her breath as the chill air struck her bare flesh. She was shuddering with the cold, and it made her hands clumsy too, so that she fumbled with the sweatshirt and pants and wrestled on a pair of thick walking socks.

She was glad there was no mirror. She had always been famous amongst her friends for her good grooming, and they would howl with laughter to see her now, but it was just too bad, Mallory thought. It was that or freeze to death, and it wasn't as if Torr was going to care.

The sound of the kitchen door opening and closing made her dive under the duvet, heart suddenly thumping. Torr and Charlie were back. Any minute now he would come in here and get into bed beside her. And then...

Then nothing, Mallory reminded herself. Ashamed of her behaviour on their wedding night, she had been prepared to try again if Torr had ever shown any interest in her, but he had made it plain that she meant as little to him as he did to her. He had even told her outright this evening that he had no intention of touching her, so there was absolutely no reason to be nervous.

Knowing that didn't stop Mallory lying tensely under the duvet, straining to hear Torr's approach over the screeching of the wind as it hurled itself at the window, making it rattle and creak alarmingly. What would be more nerve-racking? she wondered. To spend the night with Torr lying beside her, or to spend the night alone in the dark with the storm raging outside?

On the whole, Mallory decided she would be better off with Torr, but she still jumped when he pushed open the door, and she wriggled deeper under the mound of blankets and duvet until only her nose and the top of her head was showing.

CHAPTER THREE

'I GAVE Charlie a couple of biscuits, is that right?' said Torr.

'Er…yes…thanks.'

Mallory had to pull the duvet down over her mouth so that he could hear her.

'And I said goodnight, told him to have a nice sleep, and that we'd see him in the morning, the way you always do.'

Forgetting her embarrassment in surprise, Mallory pulled herself up to stare at him. 'How on earth do you know *that*?'

'It's your night-time ritual.' Torr sat down on the edge of the bed, making it dip and creak, and pulled off his boots. 'I've heard you talking to Charlie in the kitchen.'

He had been eavesdropping on her one-sided conversations with the dog all this time, and she had never known it! Mallory didn't know whether to feel foolish or astounded that he had bothered to listen. 'I suppose you think I'm a sentimental idiot?'

'No,' he said, yanking his thick Guernsey sweater over his head. 'I like the way you give him so much attention.'

It's more than you give me. The unspoken words seemed to echo round the room, as a brushed cotton shirt followed the sweater, and Mallory found her eyes resting on his broad, bare back before she remembered to yank her gaze away and huddle back down under the duvet. She wasn't supposed to be gawping at the sight of husband undressing.

She just hoped that he wasn't planning to sleep naked. She didn't know how she would cope with that. But, no, when she peeped another glance, he was wearing high-tech thermal gear that looked as if it were top of the range for climbers. She should have realised that his experience on the hills would mean that he was much better prepared for the cold than she was. Walking Charlie required boots and a good waterproof jacket, but that was as far as her outdoor equipment went.

'Thank you for taking him out,' she said belatedly.

'No problem. I like dogs.'

A silence loomed, and Mallory rushed to fill it. 'Have you ever thought about having one?' she asked, cringing a little at how breathless she sounded. If she carried on like this, Torr would guess how nervous she was.

'I had a dog called Basher when I was a boy,' Torr told her as he got to his feet and crossed over to the light switch. 'He was the best dog you could ever have. I could never replace him.'

'I feel like that about Charlie.'

The room was plunged into blackness as Torr switched off the light, and the sound of the wind and the rain seemed to intensify in the dark. Mallory shivered and forced her mind back to dogs.

Torr was feeling his way back to the bed. 'I never thought of you as a dog person,' she said, in the same thin, high voice.

'I could say the same of you.'

Annoyingly, Torr sounded exactly as normal. He pulled back the blankets on his side of the bed. 'I've always thought Charlie is an odd sort of dog for you to have.'

Bedsprings creaked and the mattress dipped alarmingly

under his weight, so that Mallory had to grab onto her side of bed to stop herself rolling towards him.

'What do you mean, odd?' she asked edgily, to take her mind off the fact that Torr was calmly getting into bed beside her.

'I suppose I was thinking about that old adage that dogs look like their owners—or is it the other way round?' He felt around for a pillow, and shifted his shoulders to make himself comfortable. 'I would have expected you to be a cat person, or if you were going to have a dog that it would be a pedigree, something elegant and a little aloof—like a saluki, perhaps. Charlie is a nice dog,' he said, 'but he doesn't fit with your image at all.'

'What *is* my image?' Mallory asked with a touch of irritation.

Torr thought about it. 'Elegant,' he said. 'Stylish…sophisticated. Not like Charlie, in fact.'

'That's just the way I dress, not the way I am,' she said sharply. 'Why do you care whether Charlie fits with my image or not anyway?'

'I don't,' said Torr, infuriatingly calm. 'I was just trying to make conversation. I thought it might distract you from the fact that we were sharing a bed.'

It had, but now that he'd mentioned it his closeness was all too noticeable. They weren't quite touching, but only because Mallory was clutching the edge of the mattress, and she was still burningly conscious of his warm solid form next to her. It reminded her all too vividly of their wedding night, when she had lain frozen with horror as Torr turned to her and the enormity of the mistake she had made hit her for the first time.

There was silence for a while. Mallory lay tensely, not wanting to move in case she brushed against him, but her foot was itching, and her legs felt cramped, so she moved them very carefully, hoping that Torr wouldn't notice. Perhaps he had fallen asleep?

'I hope you're not going to twitch all night.' His voice came out of the darkness and she started.

'I'm not twitching! I'm just trying to get comfortable.'

'I thought you were tired?'

'I was, but I think I've got past it, and now I feel all wound up again.' Mallory sighed and shifted restlessly. 'Everything's so strange. This weird place, the storm…you.'

'I'm not strange,' Torr pointed out. 'I'm your husband.'

'It's strange being in bed with you.'

It was Torr's turn to sigh. 'You can relax,' he said impatiently. 'I'm not about to try and seduce you. I've already told you that I won't lay a finger on you—unless you ask, of course,' he added.

The mockery in his voice stung Mallory. 'I can't imagine that happening!' she snapped.

'Fine,' he said. 'Be hung up on Steve. He's not worth it, but if you want to waste your life pining for a man who treated you the way he did, that's your choice. I think you're a fool, but I'm not going to waste my breath persuading you to change your mind. It's up to you, Mallory. If you ever decide that you want a proper marriage, let me know, but until then we'll carry on as we are. I'm not going to force you. I don't even *want* you, knowing that you feel the way you do about Steve, so you're quite safe from me.'

'I know,' she muttered, wishing he didn't make her feel as if she were being stupid.

'Good. Now, it's been a long day and I'm tired even if you're not, so let's try and get some sleep.' Torr turned onto his side, and the bedsprings protested as he made himself comfortable. 'Goodnight.'

'Goodnight.'

Clinging grimly to the edge of the mattress, Mallory willed herself to sleep, or, if not that, to keep still, but it was hard. Since Torr had climbed calmly into bed beside her an adrenalin rush of awareness and self-consciousness had kept her warm, but now that he had disposed of her nervousness so astringently, cold began to seep in through the layers of blankets. No matter how tightly she hugged the duvet around her neck, the draught through the window sent icy fingers creeping into the bed.

Outside, the wind howled while the rain was lashing the glass of the rickety old window in time-honoured fashion. The blackness was extraordinary. At home, there was always the glow of streetlamps, and a faint orange haze hung over the city, no matter how dark the night. She was used to the sounds of the street—heels on a pavement, laughter and arguments, cars, distant sirens. It was never completely quiet, just as it was never completely dark.

But here… It was hardly quiet, with the storm battering at the castle, but the blackness was total. Mallory wished that she had suggested Charlie sleep in the room too. He tended to snort and snuffle in his sleep, and sometimes he could be a bit whiffy, but at least she would have known that he was there.

There was Torr, of course. If only she knew him better. If only they were friends she could cuddle into him and confess that she was cold and lonely and scared. But that would only make him think that she was even more pathetic than he clearly already did.

An exasperated sigh came out of the darkness. 'For God's sake, Mallory, stop fidgeting!'

'I'm cold,' she said sullenly.

With a muttered exclamation, Torr turned over and with one brisk movement pulled Mallory into the curve of his body.

'What are you doing?' she protested breathlessly, taken unawares.

'I'm *trying* to get some sleep,' he said, his crisp voice at variance with his warm, relaxed body, 'and I'm clearly not going to get any with you either shivering with cold or vibrating away like a tuning fork because you feel tense.'

'Obviously I was right to feel tense,' muttered Mallory, making a token effort to wriggle against the firmness of his grip, until she realised that she was effectively snuggling closer to him. 'I thought you weren't going to lay a finger on me?'

'I meant for the purposes of seduction.' Torr adjusted his arm so that it fitted comfortably under her neck. His other arm lay over her waist, holding her into him. 'In case you were wondering, this is not seduction. This is strategy in the interests of a good night's sleep. We're going to roll together some time on this mattress, so we might as well get it over with. We can't spend all night hanging onto the edge of the bed.'

That was precisely what Mallory had been planning, but it didn't seem like such a good idea now that she was getting warm. Her heart was thudding still, but there was a strange comfort, too, in the hard, solid body behind her, the powerful arm over her. She could feel Torr's chest rising and falling steadily, and his breath stirred her hair. The storm seemed muted now, the cold less menacing, and the exhaustion which tension had kept at bay rolled over her once more.

'I'm not sure this is a good idea.' She managed a last protest, but it sounded feeble even to her own ears.

'Maybe it isn't, but we'll worry about that in the morning,' said Torr. His voice was deep, and very close to her ear, and an inexplicable *frisson* snaked its way down Mallory's spine. 'In the meantime,' he went on, in distinctly unloverlike tones, 'will you please shut up and go to sleep?'

Mallory opened her eyes to find herself blinking at a grimy wall. Blearily, she rolled over, but the view was no better on her back. An equally dirty ceiling and a naked lightbulb dangling from a frayed cord.

Kincaillie. Memories from the night before seeped back as she pulled herself up onto the pillows and pushed the dark, tangled hair away from her face. Driving endlessly through the dark. The wind shrieking like a banshee. Stumbling along that nightmarish passage.

Torr pulling off his shirt to reveal a broad, smooth back.

Mallory's mind stumbled at the memory and a tiny frown creased between her brows. Why remember *that* out of all the trauma of the night before?

The bitter cold… She could hardly forget that either, she thought, hurrying on mentally, or the terrifying feeling that the storm was about to burst through the window into the suffocating blackness. It was a wonder she had managed to sleep at all.

And then, of course, she remembered Torr's hands pulling her brusquely towards him, the feel of his body, hard and warm and insensibly reassuring against her, and for no reason Mallory felt her cheeks grow hot. Well, she had been tired, and more than a little frightened, and there had been no point in being cold. It wasn't as if she had snuggled into him of her own accord, was it? Torr had made it very clear that not even a smidgeon of affection had been involved.

So that was all right, then.

Wondering why she was even thinking about it, Mallory reached an arm out from beneath the duvet to retrieve her watch, and grimaced at the temperature and the time. It was late, and still very cold. Pushing back the blankets and swinging her legs out of bed took a huge effort of will, and she shivered anew as she scrabbled through her case in search of a fleece and an extra pair of socks. Not exactly a glamorous look, but it would have to do until she had had a bath.

The smell of freshly made coffee met her as she padded through to the kitchen, the flagstones chill even through two pairs of socks, and she sniffed appreciatively. It reminded her of her favourite Italian delicatessen, where she met her friends for coffee…or used to meet, she remembered bleakly. There were no friendly little places to drop in for coffee around Kincaillie, and no friends to meet.

If anything, the kitchen was more depressing in daylight than it had been the night before. It was dank and dirty and dilapidated, and the pile of boxes they had unpacked from the car the night before only added to the chaos of the scene. Mallory sighed.

The kitchen door stood open, and she went over to shut it before realising that it was just as cold inside as out, so it wasn't as if a lot of heat was being lost. Registering for the first time that the rain had stopped, Mallory stood in the doorway, hugging her arms together, and looked at her new home for the first time.

The door opened onto a walled kitchen garden, as tangled and unkempt as everything else at Kincaillie. Beyond the far wall she could see what looked like a small wood, huddled into the hollow of a forbidding hillside that reared up above them, its flanks covered with scree and heather and its top ridged with corries where snow still lay in cold white streaks.

The wind had dropped to a brisk, gusty breeze that sent clouds scudding across the sky, and the air was fresh and cold and tangy with the smell of the sea.

Torr stood on a brick path, holding a mug of coffee and watching Charlie, who was snuffling joyously around the big, messy garden, so much more interesting to him than the immaculate courtyard garden he'd been restricted to in the city. Sensing her presence, though, he looked up and barked a welcome, before bounding over to her, his tail wagging furiously.

His delight was impossible to resist, and Mallory couldn't help laughing as she bent to receive his rapturous greeting. He squirmed with delight at her attention, and, still smiling, she looked up to see that Torr had turned and was watching them both with an expression that made her heart stutter. The next instant, though, it was gone so completely that Mallory wondered if she had imagined it.

'Good morning,' she said, unaccountably shy as she straightened. It wasn't even as if they had done anything to feel shy or embarrassed about, but the memory of lying close to him, feeling him breathing, seemed suddenly startling in the cool morning air.

'Good morning.' Torr came over to join them on the paved area by the door. 'I see you managed to get some sleep, then?'

'Yes. Thank you,' said Mallory stiltedly. She had been so deeply asleep that she hadn't even stirred when he'd disentangled himself from her, and she wasn't sure if that was a good thing or a bad thing. 'Have you been up long?'

'Not really.' Torr seemed almost as awkward as she felt. 'I made some coffee, and then Charlie was keen to come out.'

'He seems to be having a good time, anyway,' she said, as Charlie bustled off in search of more smells.

'Yes.'

A ridiculously constrained silence fell.

'The water should be hot enough for a bath if you want one,' said Torr after a moment. 'I put the immersion heater on.'

'Oh. Thank you.' Mallory was torn between longing for a bath and dread at the thought of all the cleaning she would have to do first. The memory of that bathroom made her shudder. 'Er...will you keep an eye on Charlie if I go and do that now?'

'If you want, but he hardly needs watching. There are no busy roads for him to escape onto here. You don't need to worry about him now.'

'No,' said Mallory, reflecting that proximity to a busy road had also meant that they were close to central heating, immaculate plumbing, a functioning oven and all the other conveniences of modern living that had passed Kincaillie by. 'I suppose not.'

In his dark blue sweater and jeans, Torr was apparently oblivious to the cold, and said that he would stay outside with his coffee while Mallory went in to tackle the bathroom. Helping herself to a fortifying mug of coffee, she found some rubber gloves and some bleach. Torr had suggested bringing some cleaning equipment, and now she could see why. If the bathroom had seemed disgusting last night, what was it going to look like in the cold light of day?

Bracing herself, she carried the coffee down to the bathroom, took a deep breath and opened the door. And stopped dead.

The floor had been roughly swept and the bath cleared of the debris she remembered from the night before. It was still stained, and cracked with age, but it had been cleaned and rinsed, and a cloth hung neatly over the taps. Torr must have dealt with it while she was sleeping.

Mallory looked down at it thoughtfully for some moments, and then turned to inspect the basin. Like the loo, it had had a cursory clean. Not enough to make it sparkling, for sure, but at least the bathroom was usable.

Turning on the hot tap, she held her hand under it until she was sure it was going to run hot, hardly daring to believe that she would get her much longed-for bath after all. She filled the tub almost to the top, and when she lowered herself into water as hot as she could bear, she let out a long sigh of relief. The walls might still be grimy, the view through the window unremittingly bleak, but at least she was warm again. For the next few minutes that was all that mattered.

By the time she eventually made it back to the kitchen, Mallory was feeling much more herself. She had washed her hair and dried it until it fell dark and smooth and shiny to her shoulders, and was wearing black trousers and her favourite pale blue cashmere jumper.

Torr was on his knees in front of the big range, his face screwed up with effort as he reached one arm deep inside, but he looked round when Mallory came in. Something flashed in his eyes, and was quickly shuttered. 'Better?' he asked.

'Much.' Mallory hesitated. 'Thank you for cleaning the bathroom,' she said. 'I was expecting to have to do that myself.'

He hunched a shoulder, as if embarrassed. 'I thought you might want a bath this morning,' he said gruffly. 'The conditions here are worse than I remembered.'

It wasn't exactly an apology for the state of things, but Mallory sensed that he was offering an olive branch of sorts.

'I thought I'd make some more coffee,' she said, picking up the kettle. 'Do you want some?'

'Thanks.' Torr got to his feet, brushing the dust from his

hands, and showed her how to light the gas ring before resuming his awkward position practically lying half in and half out of the range.

'What are you doing?' she asked him as she retrieved the coffee from the provisions box.

'Getting this range going,' he said rather indistinctly. 'It should provide a good heat, and we'll be able to cook on it.'

He might be able to, but Mallory couldn't begin to imagine how she would begin to even boil an egg on it. She had never yearned to make jams and chutney in a farmhouse kitchen; the latest technology, preferably black and gleaming or cool stainless steel, was much more her style.

She watched him, unwillingly impressed by his competence. 'Where did you learn to do that?'

'I grew up in the country,' he told her, grunting with effort. 'We had a range in the kitchen. It wasn't as old as this, but I'm assuming the principle is the same. Ah, that's it!' he said with satisfaction, and withdrew his arm once more.

That was something else Mallory hadn't known about him before. 'I didn't have you down as a country boy,' she said. 'Did you live in Scotland?'

'No.' Torr brushed ashes from his hands. 'My father came to work in England as a young man and never moved back. But, like a lot of expatriate Scots, the longer he was away the more Scottish he became. He was always very insistent about my Scottish heritage.' His mouth quirked at one corner. 'He even named me after a loch, which I thought was taking things a bit far. You can imagine how much stick I got about being called Torridon McIver at my very English school!'

Mallory had a sudden vivid image of a boy with dark hair and dark blue eyes and a beaky, combative face. He would have squared up to his tormentors, that was for sure. It was a strange feeling to imagine him as a young boy, just as it was disconcerting to realise just how different he looked in his faded jeans and his bulky jumper. The man washing his hands at the sink was barely recognisable as the stony-faced businessman in an immaculate suit who had effectively blackmailed her into marriage.

'I'll show you round after this,' he said, as they had some bread and jam with coffee for breakfast. 'Kincaillie's your home now, so you might as well get to know it.'

How could this be home? Mallory wondered as she followed Torr along interminable passageways. Charlie trotted interestedly behind them, his claws clicking on the bare floors. They went up and down an extraordinary variety of staircases—some narrow, some grand, some stone and spiralling, some broad and wooden—and in and out of endless rooms. Not all were as dramatic as the great hall, but they were equally cheerless.

The damage wrought by a leaking roof and years of neglect and abandon was depressingly obvious, and Mallory was baffled by the warmth in Torr's voice as he ran a hand over a piece of stonework, or pointed out a view from one of the windows, almost as if he didn't see the damp and the dirt and the dust and the debris. She might grimace at patches of mould or rusty streaks, but he seemed able to picture the rooms as they had once been, when Kincaillie was a living, working house rather than a crumbling ruin.

Some of the rooms still had occasional pieces of furniture, shrouded in dust sheets, and they came across the odd stag's head, stuffed and rotting on the wall, but otherwise the place was eerily bare.

'What happened to the rest of the stuff?' Mallory asked, peering underneath a dust sheet to find a massive table with great carved legs that looked as if it had been simply too heavy to move.

'When my great-uncle finally went into a home, his son had all the pictures, silver and the best pieces of furniture put into storage. I'll bring them back, but not until I've done some repairs.'

'*Some* repairs?' Mallory dropped the sheet and straightened to stare at him. 'Torr, this place is practically a ruin!' She waved an arm at the crumbling grandeur around them. 'It would take for ever to restore all this.'

Torr shrugged. 'One thing I've got now is time.'

'But have you got the money? It'll cost a fortune just to tackle a fraction of what needs to be done.'

'I know that,' he said, unperturbed. 'I made a lot of money from selling my businesses, but I've no intention of spending unnecessarily. There's inheritance tax to be taken into account, and I've made a number of investments for the future, so I haven't got unlimited funds to do up Kincaillie. That's why I'm planning to do as much as possible myself.'

She gaped at him. 'You're not serious?'

'Of course I'm serious,' he said a little irritably. 'Why wouldn't I be?'

'But…how will you know what to do?'

Torr shrugged. 'Construction was my business,' he reminded her.

Mallory was having trouble reconciling the idea of the sharp-suited businessman he had always seemed to be doing heavy building work. She was also uncomfortably aware that he would have another quarter of a million pounds to spend on Kincaillie if he hadn't settled all *her* debts.

'I always thought of you in an office, wheeling and dealing,' she said.

'I didn't spend much time on site latterly, that's true,' he said, 'but I started out doing my own properties, developing them and selling them on. I'm looking forward to working with my hands again.'

He looked assessingly around the room, as if working out how he would tackle it. 'I can't do everything, of course. The roof is the biggest expense, but it's critical to get the place weatherproof as soon as possible, so I've got contractors coming to replace the whole roof in a couple of weeks. I'll get other contractors in for the rewiring and damp-proofing too, as they're both big jobs, but the joinery, the plastering and all the rest I can do myself.'

'I think it's madness,' said Mallory frankly. 'Even if you had limitless funds to get someone else to do all the work it would be a crazy project, but to consider doing it yourself…' She shook her head, overwhelmed by the enormity of the task he had set himself. 'It's more than crazy,' she told him. 'It's irresponsible.'

'In what way?' Torr's voice, which had warmed as he showed her round, was frosted with ice once more.

'It's a huge risk, and you know it!'

'I like risks.'

His calm confidence riled Mallory. There was something arrogant about a man like Torr who refused to accept his own limitations. 'And what am I supposed to do while you're wasting your life on this crazy scheme?'

'Help?' he suggested sardonically.

The air was simmering with a familiar hostility, as if the unspoken truce of the previous night had evaporated, leached away by the echoing stone walls. Torr's dark blue eyes were cool once more, but Mallory met them squarely, her own bright with defiance.

'Doing what?' she demanded. 'I don't know anything about building. I can do you a fabulous decorative scheme, but it would be a very long time before you'll be in a position to think about colour scheme, even if you got in a whole fleet of builders.'

Torr was unimpressed. 'There's lots of basic work to be done. You don't need to be trained to clear a room of rubbish, and you could always learn how to plaster and tile. There's the garden to be cleared, too. I think you'll find there's plenty you could do if you put your mind to it.'

'I didn't realise that I was expected to do hard labour as part of our deal!' Mallory said snippily, before she could help herself.

There was a dangerously white look around Torr's mouth, and he was clearly having difficulty keeping his temper in check. 'Our *deal,*' he said icily, 'was marriage. You're my wife, and all I expect from you is that you share in this project. It's something we should be able to do together.'

'It's not something we discussed together though, is it? *You* decided to come all on your own, even though you knew this was the last place I'd want to be.'

'And *you* chose to come with me,' said Torr, his voice as hard as his expression.

'You know why—' Mallory began defensively, but he interrupted her with a dismissive gesture of his hand.

'The reasons don't matter. You made a choice, Mallory,' he said. 'Now live with it.'

Live with it. Mallory hunched her shoulders and turned up the collar of her jacket as she set off to take Charlie for a walk, leaving Torr to start cleaning the kitchen so they could unpack.

After that unpleasant exchange they had cut short the tour. There was still a rabbit warren of attic rooms to explore, but

Mallory had seen enough. She wasn't surprised the previous Laird had chosen to emigrate to New Zealand. No one in their right mind would want to make home here, she thought. Kincaillie was a dump, a crumbling, rotting pile of old stones.

And she was going to have to live with it.

Mallory dug her hands in her pockets and trudged after Charlie. She needed some time alone. The wind whipped her dark hair about her face and made her narrow her eyes. The earlier brightness had been swallowed up by lowering grey clouds, and although it wasn't exactly raining, there was a kind of fine mizzle in the air that clung to her skin.

It didn't take long to cross the tussocky grass of the promontory and find the sea. Charlie was delighted to discover a beach, and plunged straight into the water. He loved the sea and would frolic in and out of waves for hours if she let him.

Mallory scrambled over the rocks down to the shoreline rather more slowly, and walked along the beach, her feet crunching on the fine shingle. It had a faint pink tinge to it, and when she stopped and looked more closely she could see that it was made up of millions of crushed shells.

At the end of the beach, Mallory sat on a lichen-stained rock to watch Charlie play. Torr had been right when he'd said that the dog would love it here. Holding her hair back from her face as best as she could, she breathed in the air, salty and seaweedy and laced with the heathery smell of the hills. The sea was a sullen grey, choppy in the stiff breeze, and she could just make out the blurry grey outlines of the Western Isles on the horizon. Sea birds flitted around the rocks and wheeled, screeching, over the sea, but she didn't recognise any of them.

She didn't recognise *anything* about this place, Mallory realised. The forbidding castle behind her, with its backdrop of looming, brooding mountains, the distant islands shrouded in mysterious mist, this strange pink beach, the silence broken only by the wind and the bubbling, croaking, piping cries of the birds around her… It was hard to imagine anywhere more different from the bustling centre of Ellsborough, with its people and shops and restaurants. *That* was home.

Mallory shivered and huddled into her jacket. This was an awful place. Bleak, harsh, cold. Unwelcoming. Intimidating.

It made Mallory feel very small and very lonely, and all at once she was overwhelmed with it all. What was she doing here? She should be in her lovely little house, or out at work, meeting clients, flipping through fabrics and wallpaper samples, putting together design boards. She should be meeting a friend for lunch, or popping down to the delicatessen for some of its wonderful cheeses. She should be looking forward to the evening, to welcoming Steve home and knowing that they had the whole night and a whole lifetime together to come.

She should be planning her wedding.

She should be happy.

Instead she was here, trapped at Kincaillie with a man who didn't love her—who didn't even want her.

CHAPTER FOUR

MALLORY'S heart tore.

Instinctively, she reached for the diamond around her neck. The necklace represented a memory of the times when she had been completely happy, the dream that Steve would come back and she would be happy again, the hope that somehow everything would work out. Whenever her wretchedness threatened to become unbearable she would clutch it for comfort, but there was no comfort now.

Sitting on that cold, lonely beach, Mallory felt reality hit for the first time. Steve had gone. He wasn't coming back. It was over.

He had betrayed her and abandoned her, and all those golden memories were worthless now. There would be no happy ending, with him riding out of the sunset to rescue her from Torridon McIver with a convincing explanation for what he had done. He wouldn't be making it all right.

And that meant that there was nothing for her to dream about any more, nothing to hope for. She was left with the desolation of trudging across a tundra of hopelessness, without even the comfort of knowing what she wanted any more.

Mallory pulled the chain out from under her jumper and

unfastened it so that she could look at it properly. It felt light and insubstantial on her palm. She stared down at it for a long time. When Steve had given it to her she had thought that it was the most beautiful and precious thing she had ever owned, but out here, surrounded by all this savage grandeur, it looked suddenly tawdry and cold, meaningless, like all her other memories now.

Abruptly, Mallory closed her hand around the necklace and jumped off the rock to walk down to where the waves were breaking on the shingle. Uncurling her fingers, she took a last look before hurling it as far as she could out into the sea. There was a tiny wink as the diamond caught the light, and then it was gone.

Charlie, thinking that she had thrown a stick, barked excitedly and plunged in after it, but the necklace, like Steve, had disappeared without a trace.

For a long moment Mallory stood frozen, aghast at what she had done, and then all at once she started to cry.

It was the first time she had cried, cried properly, since Steve had disappeared that terrible day. Up to now she had kept the bitterness and the misery and the humiliation and the pain locked tightly inside her, sealing it in ice. It had kept her cold ever since, but she had almost welcomed the numbness. Better to feel nothing than to feel the ragged, wrenching pain of betrayal.

'Let it all out,' friends had advised, but Mallory wouldn't. *Couldn't.* She'd been terrified that once she started she wouldn't be able to stop, that the tears would dissolve the ice and let the hurt out, and if that happened, Mallory hadn't known how she would stop herself from falling apart completely.

Now the misery she had kept bottled up for so long erupted

with terrifying force. It was even more painful than Mallory had imagined—and, just as she had feared, once she had started she didn't seem to be able to stop crying, great jagged, wrenching sobs that felt as if they were tearing her apart.

Sinking down onto the shingle, she howled at the uncaring sea, until Charlie, puzzled and concerned by her distress, came over to paw at her and whine.

'It's all right... I'm all right,' she gasped through her tears, trying to reassure him, but Charlie knew that she wasn't all right. He pushed closer to lick her face, and she put her arms round him and buried her face in his wet fur, weeping out her loneliness and her pain and her grief for everything that she had lost until she was raw and aching inside.

But strangely, when the racking sobs eventually subsided, Mallory felt much calmer than at any time since Steve had left her. She wiped her cheeks with her palms and drew shuddering breaths, testing herself gingerly. Her ribs hurt, and her heart felt as if it had done ten rounds with a champion boxer, but, yes, she felt better, lighter somehow.

Mallory let out a long, wavering sigh and got up from the shingle, brushing the tiny pieces of shell from her hands. Charlie looked up at her expectantly. His joy in the water had been muted by her tears, and now he stuck close beside her, waiting to see what she was going to do next.

'Good question,' said Mallory, as if he had asked it out loud. She turned to look at Kincaillie. It looked as inhospitable as ever, but they had nowhere else to go.

'We'll finish our walk,' she told him, 'but then we'll have to go back.'

Torr was emptying ashes onto the kitchen garden when she and Charlie came back through the gate at last, and her heart jumped a little at the sight of him. She needed to talk to him, but she hadn't counted on facing him just yet. Not until she had made herself look a little more presentable at least.

There had been a peaty brown burn running down the beach, and she had splashed some of its freezing water onto her face, but it was hard to disguise the effects of a crying jag, and knowing that she was bug-eyed and blotchy made her feel at a disadvantage before she had even started. Perhaps Torr would be a gentleman and pretend not to notice?

A frown touched Torr's eyes as he straightened to look at Mallory more closely. 'You've been crying,' he said.

Embarrassed, she slid her gaze away from his. 'I've been thinking.' She tried to correct him.

'About Steve?'

'Yes,' she admitted. 'And about being here, being married to you...' She swallowed, not sure how to express the thoughts that had been churning round her head as she walked Charlie. 'I think we need to talk,' she said at last.

Something shifted in Torr's expression. 'Now?'

'If you've got a moment,' she said awkwardly. Having got this far, she might as well get it over with. Torr could only say no to her idea, after all, and even if he did she would be no worse off than she was now.

'Time is something I've got plenty of,' said Torr, upending the bucket to get rid of the last of the ash on the tangled and overgrown bed where fruit bushes still struggled to survive. 'There are no deadlines here,' he said. 'Shall we go in? I got the range going, but there won't be much heat yet. It might be a bit warmer than out here, though.'

They made yet more coffee, so at least they had something hot to hold, and sat on either side of the kitchen table.

'So,' said Torr. 'I imagine you're going to tell me that you don't want to stay.'

Mallory looked down at her mug. 'I do want to leave, yes, but I know that I can't.'

'You're not a prisoner!'

'Not literally, but I might as well be,' she said, lifting her eyes to meet his scowl. 'I owe you a lot of money, Torr. That was why I married you.'

'Do you think I don't know that?' he asked harshly. 'You don't owe me anything, Mallory. The money was part of the deal.'

'I know, and that's why I can't walk away, even though I hate it here and would rather be almost anywhere else,' she said frankly. 'I can't end our marriage the way I want to unless I can repay that money, and I'm never going to be able to do that if I stay here.'

She had spoken without thinking, and Torr didn't answer immediately. He was studying his coffee, head bent and dark brows contracted in a frown.

For some reason Mallory could hear her words echoing in the silence. *I hate it here…hate it…hate it…end our marriage the way I want to…end our marriage…end…* In retrospect, they sounded more brutal than she had intended. Just as well Torr didn't love her either, or it would have been an uncomfortable moment.

The pause went on for so long that it began to feel uncomfortable anyway, but just as she was about to break it Torr lifted his head and looked straight across at her. His eyes were very blue and penetrating as they met hers, and Mallory's pulse gave a strange little kick.

'So what are you suggesting?' he asked.

It was Mallory who looked away first. For a moment there she had forgotten what she wanted to say. 'That I work off my debt,' she told him. 'I saw how much work there is to do here this morning. If you really are going to do it yourself, you're going to need help and, as you pointed out, there are things I could do. I might not be much use with the plumbing or the electricity, but I can clean and I can paint, and I can learn to do other things too, just like you said.'

'And in exchange?'

She drew a breath. It had seemed a good idea when she was walking by the sea, but she had no idea how Torr was going to react. Well, she wouldn't know unless she put it to him.

'If I work here for a year, doing whatever you need me to do, I would like you to give me a divorce at the end of it and consider our debt settled.'

'You want to earn a divorce?' Torr's voice was empty of all inflexion, and Mallory squirmed a little.

'Yes. I realise that I'm asking you to be generous,' she said carefully, 'but I would work really hard, and if I knew I could leave eventually I wouldn't complain about the conditions here. I'd help you as much as I could.'

'I see,' said Torr, his expression still impossible to read. 'And if I agree to this?'

'I'd go back to Ellsborough.'

'To do what?'

'I don't know,' she admitted. 'I just know that the thought of being stuck here for ever is unendurable.' She looked around her at the dirty, dilapidated kitchen. 'This place… Kincaillie…it's awful,' she tried to explain. 'It would be awful even if it wasn't falling down. There's nothing to do here, no one to see, nowhere to go. I can't live here long-term, but I can bear it for a year.'

'So you're not planning to go in search of Steve?' Torr said.

She flushed. 'No,' she said. Picking up a teaspoon, she stirred her coffee mindlessly. 'I suppose that somewhere deep inside I was holding onto the hope that Steve would come and rescue me from you,' she confessed, dark hair swinging forward to hide her face.

'Just like in a fairy tale,' he commented sardonically.

'A bit,' she agreed. 'But he's not going to come.'

'No,' said Torr, and Mallory sighed.

'I just realised that this morning. It's taken until now for me to understand properly that I'm on my own now. That means I'm going to have to rescue myself, and until I do I'm stuck with you.'

'Charmingly put!' he said sardonically.

Mallory's flush deepened and she set her teeth. 'I'm sorry, but I think it's better if we're honest with each other. There was never any pretence that marriage meant anything more than a practical arrangement to either of us, was there? Our marriage doesn't mean any more to you than it does to me,' she reminded him.

'The situation has changed since we made our deal,' she went on. 'You're certainly not going to be doing any entertaining for a while, so you hardly need a hostess. If you had known that you were going to inherit Kincaillie you would have married someone quite different, wouldn't you?'

'Would I?'

'There's no reason you shouldn't marry again when we're divorced,' Mallory reassured him, assuming that he was being sarcastic, but Torr sat back in his chair and regarded her coolly across the table.

'I haven't agreed to a divorce yet,' he pointed out.

Mallory bit her lip. 'You can't want me to stay,' she said cajolingly. 'We would just make each other miserable. Imagine what it would be like to be stuck here, with just the two of us hating each other more and more because neither of us is the person we really want them to be,' she said. 'It would be unbearable for both of us.'

'If you say so.' Torr's expression was indecipherable.

Mallory pushed her hair behind her ears. He was making her work for it, she realised. Well, that was OK. She would have to find another way to persuade him. She would do whatever it took to get back to Ellsborough and a life that she recognised, even if it wasn't the one she had wanted and thought she would have with Steve.

'I thought it all through on my walk with Charlie just now,' she started. 'I've been wretched about Steve for too long. It's awful being that unhappy,' she told him. 'You can't think clearly about anything. If I'd been thinking, I'd never have married you, but I got myself into this mess, and that means I'm going to have to find a way out of it—even if it does mean putting in a year of hard labour out here.

'I'm not expecting you to just let me walk away from everything I owe you,' she said to Torr, meeting his eyes directly across the table, her own a deep, dark brown. 'I agreed to marry you, and that means I owe you more than money. I owe you some support too. I think you're mad, but if you're determined to stay here and restore this place, I'll stay with you and help you in every way I can.'

'And then you'll go?' said Torr.

'Yes, then I'll go,' Mallory agreed. 'It's the best solution for both of us, Torr.'

He lifted a sardonic brow. 'Is it?'

'I think so. You don't want to be stuck out here for years with only a reluctant, complaining wife for company, do you?'

'Not when you put it like that, no.'

'And I want to go home,' she said. 'But I want to earn the right to do that, too. It's not just about money,' she tried to explain. 'Over the last few months I've lost everything, and one of the most important things I've lost is my self-respect. I need to find that again,' she told Torr, her brown eyes clear and resolute.

Torr held her gaze for a long, long moment and then he looked away. 'All right,' he said abruptly. 'We'll do it your way. We'll work together on Kincaillie. If we've made real progress in a year's time, and you still want to go, I'll divorce you and we'll consider your debts settled in full. Does that seem fair?'

'Very fair,' said Mallory, relieved. 'Thank you.'

Until then she hadn't realised just how tense she had been, but her shoulders relaxed as she let out a long breath and smiled gratefully at him. 'You won't regret it,' she promised. 'I won't ask you for anything else. I won't complain about the conditions. I won't nag you about going home. I'll be a perfect wife, in fact,' she said without thinking, and immediately wished she hadn't when Torr's brows lifted mockingly.

'A perfect wife?' he echoed. 'Really?'

Damn. What had she said that for? Mallory wondered, vexed with herself. She had only been trying to lighten the atmosphere a little. Now she could practically hear him thinking that perfect wives didn't shrink away when their husbands touched them.

Discomfited, she bit her lip. 'The perfect housekeeper, then,' she amended. 'And, given the state of this place, I'd say you need one of those more than you need someone to sleep with!'

'I'm sure you're right,' said Torr, with one of his looks.

There was a funny, fizzling little pause. 'Well,' said Mallory brightly after a moment, 'if I'm going to earn my divorce, I'd better get on with it! What would you like me to do first?'

Torr drained his coffee and pushed back his chair. 'Let's finish cleaning in here first,' he said. 'We may as well make our living quarters comfortable before we start on the rest of the castle.'

He had already made a start while she was walking Charlie, but the kitchen was so big that it still took the two of them the rest of the afternoon to make an impression on it, and even then it was far from finished. Together they dusted and brushed and scrubbed and rinsed and wiped, until Torr suggested they stop for a cup of tea.

Mallory agreed with alacrity. Having insisted that she wanted to work off her debts, she had had to wait for Torr to stop work first.

'At least this end is clean enough to unpack some of our stuff,' she said, sitting back on her heels and wringing her cloth into a bucket. 'These cupboards here are as clean as they're going to get.'

'We'll do that after tea, then we might as well call it a day.'

'OK.' Mallory got to her feet and stretched. She was tired and dirty and stiff, but strangely she felt better too. There must be something therapeutic about cleaning, she decided, and working side by side with Torr had been much easier than she'd expected. They had cleaned in silence, apart from occasional requests to pass over a dustpan and brush, or offers to fetch more hot water, but it hadn't been uncomfortable, she realised in some surprise.

She was very glad now that she had plucked up the courage to talk to him before she had had a chance to lose her nerve about the idea of earning a divorce. She had wondered how Torr would react, and she still wasn't really sure what he thought, but he had agreed. That was the main thing.

The discussion had cleared the air, too. Now they both

knew where they stood, and that meant that some of that terrible tension had seeped out of the atmosphere. Mallory didn't mind getting dirty now that she knew that she would be able to leave eventually. She even welcomed the idea of pushing herself physically so that she would be too tired to think about Steve.

That had been her mistake, she decided. She should have kept herself busy before now, instead of retreating into a frozen state where even the smallest activity was an effort of will.

Well, that would change, Mallory resolved. She was tired of feeling powerless and wretched. From now on she would just think about the next job to be done.

Now that she wasn't feeling so trapped, she could even see that there might be some satisfaction in bringing the castle back to life. It would certainly be a challenge, if not the ultimate displacement activity. It could be a healing process, she mused. If she threw herself into the project for a year, by the time she left she would be stronger, steadier and ready to face the world again. She could go back to Ellsborough with her head up and her pride intact.

Perhaps Torr would have changed his mind about staying by then. The restoration of Kincaillie was a massive project— surely too much for one man?

Not that Torr was the type to admit it. Mallory couldn't imagine him ever giving up once he had decided to do something.

She watched him out of the corner of her eye as she collected up their cleaning materials. He was lighting a gas ring, his fingers deft with the matches, and she was struck anew by how competent he was, how reassuringly solid and immediate. All she could see of him was the austere profile, his brows drawn together in concentration as he adjusted the flame, but as her gaze travelled unthinkingly down to the stern mouth she suddenly found herself remembering the feel of his body the night before, and an unaccountable little *frisson* snaked its way down her spine.

As if that weren't disconcerting enough, Torr chose that moment to lift his eyes without warning and caught her watching him. Mallory's heart gave a strange little jerk, but it was only when she saw his brows lift in an unspoken question that she realised that she was staring at him.

Oddly shaken, she wrenched her gaze away and cleared her throat.

'Why are you using the gas ring?' She asked the first question that came into her head. Well, she had to think of *some* reason to explain why she'd been watching her own husband. 'I thought you'd got the range working?'

'I cleaned it out and lit it this morning, but it will take a good eighteen hours for the heat to come up. We'll just have to use the gas rings tonight.'

'I could make some pasta,' Mallory offered, busying herself wiping a non-existent smear off the front of a cupboard door so she didn't have to look at him directly. They had heated up some soup for lunch, but she was starving now. 'We can boil the pasta on one ring and make the sauce on the other.'

'Sounds good to me,' said Torr.

They sat at the table to drink their tea, but for some reason constraint had seeped back into the air, and Mallory was absurdly conscious of Torr sitting opposite her. She couldn't understand why. Nothing had changed. He looked just the same. The same dark features, the same blue eyes, the same mouth...

Why start noticing his mouth now, when she had never

noticed it particularly before? It had just been a mouth, but now it was as if she couldn't take her eyes off it, which was absurd. It was still just a mouth. There was nothing special about it at all, she pointed out stringently to herself.

Torr wasn't even *smiling*. He was just sitting there, drinking his tea, and if he was feeling awkward he certainly didn't show it. That only made Mallory edgier than ever.

She was glad when she had finished her tea and could get up to start unpacking some of the boxes they had brought with them. She stored the contents neatly in the newly cleaned cupboards, which was really quite satisfying. Torr let her get on with it while he laid the fire again. It was dark by then, and the flickering flames gave an illusion of warmth and cheerfulness even if the heat they gave out did little to alleviate the chill of the vast kitchen unless you were sitting right in front of it.

Fortunately, the cleaning had kept Mallory warm enough, but she was feeling decidedly grubby by the time she had finished, and was glad to take off her cleaning clothes and have the first bath. Torr bathed later, while she made a simple sauce to go with the pasta. She had found her iPod when unpacking the kitchen equipment, and it was amazing how comforting it was to have familiar music in the background as she cooked. If she carried on like this she would start feeling at home, Mallory thought wryly.

After supper they sat in the armchairs on either side of the fire, just as they had done the night before. Mallory kept her eyes on the flames and tried not to think about going to bed with Torr again—because whenever she did she found herself getting ridiculously nervous. At least last night she had been too tired to care where she slept, but it was different now. She had just convinced herself that her strange awareness of Torr had been no more than a momentary aberration when he came in after his bath. His hair was wet, and he was wearing a clean jumper and jeans, and her stomach did that funny little flip again.

Something else to put down to tiredness and the strangeness of living in a ruined castle, Mallory decided firmly. No wonder she was imagining things in this bizarre place.

'Here,' said Torr, handing Mallory a glass.

'What is it?' she asked, eyeing the golden liquid in surprise.

'Whisky. This is the best malt there is,' he added as he sat back down in his chair, 'so don't chuck it back. I just thought we should toast our first day at Kincaillie.'

Mallory's smile was a little twisted, but she lifted her glass. 'Here's to living with our choices,' she said in a dry voice, and then Torr did something totally unexpected.

He smiled.

'To living with it,' he echoed, and toasted her in return.

Thrown by the suddenness of his smile, Mallory took a bigger sip of whisky than she'd intended, and promptly started coughing and spluttering as the liquid burned her throat.

'I told you not to gulp it,' Torr admonished her.

'Sorry,' she croaked.

Eyes watering, she stared into the fire. Better that he thought her a reckless drinker than guessed just why she had gulped his precious whisky. Who would have thought that a simple stretch of the lips, a mere curve of the mouth, could be quite so startling?

She supposed it was because she was so unused to seeing Torr smile. There was something daunting about his usual expression, so forbiddingly unreadable, that when he had smiled just now it had been like looking at a stranger. His eyes had gleamed and his cheeks had creased, revealing strong white teeth and warming his expression in a way that left her feeling really quite…strange.

Mallory took another sip of whisky. She could feel it sliding down her throat, its warmth spreading out from her stomach. That would explain the peculiar tingle underneath her skin, anyway, and the way her cheeks felt as if they were burning.

She slid a sidelong glance from under her lashes at Torr on the other side of the fire. He was watching the flames too, legs stretched comfortably out in front of him and one hand loosely clasping his glass on the arm of the chair. He looked quite relaxed, Mallory thought enviously, as if it were perfectly normal to be sitting here in this draughty old kitchen while the entire castle crumbled about his ears.

Outside, the wind was picking up again, but here in the kitchen the only sounds were the spit and crackle of the burning logs and Charlie's sighs of contentment from the hearthrug as he hogged the best of the fire.

'Are you serious about doing most of the restoration work on your own?' Mallory broke the silence abruptly, jerking Torr out of his abstraction, and he glanced across at her.

'I won't be on my own now,' he pointed out. 'You're going to help me.'

'Only for a year,' she reminded him.

'Ah, yes.' Torr resumed his study of the fire. 'Well, a year is a long time. We can make a good start.'

'What will you do when you finish? If you ever do, of course! Sell it?'

He shook his head. 'The estate is entailed, so I couldn't sell it if I wanted to. No, I'm going to make Kincaillie the best and most exclusive hotel in Scotland.'

'A hotel?' Mallory couldn't help laughing. 'You've got to be joking! Who on earth would pay to come here?'

'You'd be surprised,' said Torr, a slight edge to his voice. 'You may not appreciate peace and quiet and stunning scenery, but I can assure you that lots of people do. Kincaillie will be *the* place for those who want to get away from it all. There'll be no gimmicks, no deals, just style and exceptional comfort, superb food and impeccable service in a wonderful setting. Oh, yes, people will come—and the more exclusive we make it, the more they'll pay,' he added confidently.

He cocked an eyebrow at Mallory. 'So, you see, I'll need your talent for interior design eventually.'

Mallory thought of the damp, dismal rooms she had seen that afternoon. It was hard to imagine ever getting to the decorating stage, but what a challenge it would be! In spite of herself, she felt a flicker of interest.

She sipped her whisky thoughtfully. 'You'd need proper building plans,' she warned.

'I know,' he said. 'I'm going to see an architect in Inverness next week. She's worked on a number of innovative restoration projects, and comes highly recommended, so I've asked her to do a preliminary design. She's been here to do a survey, and I want to go and see her initial ideas.'

'Can I come?' asked Mallory, brightening at the prospect of a trip away from Kincaillie.

He looked surprised. 'I didn't think you'd be that interested.'

'I'm interested in the idea of a town,' she said, 'and I certainly don't want to be left here on my own!'

'Of course you can come, if you want, but you may have to get used to the idea of staying on your own sometimes,' he warned. 'We can't spend the whole year without ever having a night apart. Anyone would think we were married,' he finished dryly.

Mallory sat up straighter in her chair. 'You don't really expect me to spend the night here on my own, do you?'

'You'd have Charlie for company,' said Torr.

'In case it's escaped your notice, Charlie's just a dog!'

'He'd be protection against any intruders—not that you're likely to get any round here.'

'It's not intruders I'm worried about,' said Mallory, a tart edge to her voice. 'At least a burglar would be some human company!'

'You're not telling me that you really believe in ghosts, are you?' Torr said with a touch of exasperation. 'I thought you were just being silly last night.'

'No, I don't believe in ghosts. It's everything else that makes me nervous. I'm a city girl. I hate the isolation. The silence. I can't tell you how much I long for the sound of a siren, or of someone's door banging, or the neighbours shouting! And those mountains give me the creeps.' She shuddered, thinking about the hills looming above them. 'They're so bleak and so big... Don't they make you feel trapped?'

'No,' said Torr. 'I feel trapped in a city. The hills and the sea make me feel free.'

'It doesn't look as if we've got much in common, does it?' Mallory said with a painful smile.

Torr looked down at the glass he was clasping loosely between his hands. 'No,' he said in a flat voice. 'It doesn't.'

They finished their whisky in silence.

CHAPTER FIVE

TORR wanted to begin drawing up detailed specifications for the restoration work the next morning. He told Mallory that he was planning to work his way methodically from room to room, an exercise that was clearly going to take some time.

'Do you want to come with me?' he asked her. 'It would give you an idea of what needs to be done over the next year.'

'Since I'll clearly be living here for that year, I think I would rather finish cleaning these rooms first,' said Mallory. 'We may as well make ourselves as comfortable as possible before we start on the rest of the castle.'

'OK.' Torr's shrug was indifferent. 'I'll see you for lunch.'

Mallory was glad to be left on her own. She hadn't slept well. She had been so tired by the time they went to bed that she had expected to fall asleep instantly, but, again, it hadn't worked out like that. She had been too aware of Torr beside her in a bed that seemed to have shrunk in size since the night before.

It was ridiculous, Mallory told herself crossly as she set off with Charlie into the brisk morning. She and Torr had cleared the air. They had come to an agreement about their marriage with no possibility of misunderstandings.

She had even wondered if it might be possible for them to

become friends. It seemed sensible to try. The year to come would be a lot easier if they were able to get along together. Mallory was very conscious that she hadn't made the effort to get to know Torr before, but that would change, she vowed. Now that she knew she wasn't trapped for a lifetime, she was quite prepared to look for the best in him.

Already he seemed more approachable. He had changed since he came to Kincaillie, Mallory thought. He was never going to be a golden laughing charmer like Steve, but he had shown that he was capable of being thoughtful and even kind, and for the first time she had realised that a certain dry humour underlaid some of his dour remarks.

She still didn't understand why Torr had married her in the first place. True, he had done a lot of entertaining in Ellsborough, and she had been a stylish hostess for him. Mallory could even see that she had been good for his image in lots of ways. But surely a man like Torr could have found a more willing wife to make life comfortable for him?

Of course he had said that he couldn't be bothered with emotions, and a more loving wife would probably have expected rather more romance than he had been prepared to offer, or even pretend, but surely Torr must be regretting now that he had ended up with someone quite so incompatible?

Not that he was the kind of man who would admit that he had made a mistake. The more Mallory thought about it, the more likely it seemed that Torr must be secretly relieved at the prospect of ending their marriage amicably in a year's time, with face saved on both sides. It would certainly explain how easily she had been able to persuade him to let her go. He couldn't really want her any more than she wanted him.

So there was absolutely no reason for her to feel awkward about going to bed that night. No reason to lie, twitchy and self-conscious, when Torr wished her goodnight in a neutral voice, turned on his side and fell asleep.

Mallory was left to listen resentfully to him breathing. It wasn't fair that he could fall asleep so easily when she couldn't relax. That dip in the wretched mattress meant that she had to cling tenaciously to her side of the bed to stop rolling against him, but it was bitterly cold still, and the warmth of his body was dangerously inviting. She couldn't snuggle into him, though. Somehow it seemed more uncomfortable now that there was the possibility that they might be friends than when she had been certain that she disliked him.

Torr was lying with his back to her, but she could tell from his slow, steady breathing that he was asleep. At least, she thought he was. Resolve wavering, Mallory listened harder, but his breathing was slow and steady. He was definitely asleep, she told herself. He wouldn't notice if she froze on the edge of the bed or if she moved a bit nearer.

Decision made, Mallory inched closer to his warm bulk. The mattress sagged, and the old bedsprings creaked rustily when she moved, and she held her breath, but Torr didn't stir.

Snuggling into his back with relief, she pulled the duvet tight around her so that she was cocooned in warmth, and then, because she didn't know what else to do with it, she put her arm over him and rested her hand on his chest. She could feel it rising and falling beneath her palm. He had washed his hair in the bath, and it smelt clean and fresh and vaguely lemony. She could smell soap on his skin, too, overlaid with a faint hint of woodsmoke from the fire.

Torn between the luxury of feeling warm and her disquieting awareness of Torr's nearness, Mallory spent another night drifting in and out of sleep. Every time she surfaced she was aware with a tiny shock that she was still pressed against him, but a sleepy part of her brain would remind her that it was only because she was cold, so that was all right.

Once, though, she woke with a start when he stirred and turned over. She had to quickly turn too, or she would have ended up face to face with him. The next moment she froze as Torr pulled her back into the shelter of his body and kissed her shoulder, just where it curved into her throat, mumbling something unintelligible.

Every cell in her body jumped in shock at the touch of his mouth on her skin, and Mallory inhaled sharply, but Torr was still sound asleep. There was no embarrassed apology, no hasty pulling away. Instead he wrapped his arm closer around her, holding her tight against him, and buried his face in her hair with a slumbering sigh.

So.

Mallory lay very still. Now what? *She* could disentangle herself and push him away, but that might wake him up, and that really would be awkward. It was obvious that he had just reached for her out of instinct. He probably thought that she was somebody else—another woman he was used to sharing his bed with.

Who?

The question jolted Mallory out of her slumber. Still held close into the curve of his body, she lay turning it over in her mind. Who exactly was Torr expecting to find lying next to him in bed?

His ex-wife? It seemed unlikely. Torr had been divorced for ten years, and from the little he had said she had gathered that the marriage hadn't been a matter of grand passion on either side.

So it must be someone who'd been in his life more recently. They had lived such separate lives since they were married that Torr could easily have been having a passionate affair without her having any idea, Mallory realised. But if he was in love with someone else, why marry *her*?

It could only mean that the other woman wasn't free, she decided. Perhaps she was married, or she might have ended the relationship for reasons of her own. For the first time Mallory wondered whether Torr too knew the pain of rejection. Could it be that beneath that unyielding exterior he also knew how it felt to have his heart broken?

The more she thought about it, the more it made sense. It would explain why he smiled so rarely, and why he had decided on a loveless marriage. Inheriting Kincaillie could have been just the impetus he needed to try and break free of painful memories.

Hadn't he said as much when he'd told her that they were going to Scotland? Mallory remembered. *It will be a fresh start for both of us,* he had said. *God knows, we both need it.*

She had been so wrapped up in her own misery over Steve that it had never occurred to her that Torr might be suffering too. Lying tucked into his side, craving his warmth, Mallory felt ashamed of herself. She had never used to be so self-absorbed. Wretchedness had made her boring and selfish, and it was time she stopped.

If Torr *was* unhappy, that would certainly explain why he had chosen to throw himself into the enormous task of restoring Kincaillie—such an unlikely project for a man as hard-headed and realistic as he was. Instead of wallowing in his misery, the way she had done, he had obviously chosen to set himself such a difficult goal that he simply wouldn't have time to think about what he was missing, just as she had decided to do earlier that day.

Without being aware of it, Mallory started to relax.

Knowing that she might not be the only one hurting made things easier somehow. Torr might understand more than she thought, and if he was finding it hard to let go of a dream he had lost...well, she was the last person to blame him for that. Perhaps, after all, they had more in common than she had thought.

Torr's breath stirred her hair, and his arm was heavy over her, pinning her against him and effectively making it impossible for her to move without waking, but it wasn't uncomfortable. Mallory decided to forget about moving away. If they were going to keep sleeping on this mattress, she would just have to get used to it.

She would have to get used to a lot of things over the next year, so she might as well make a start.

The restless night took its toll the next morning. Mallory woke feeling jaded. She found herself watching Torr more closely, wondering if she was right in her assumptions, but as usual he gave nothing away. If he did have a broken heart, he was hiding it pretty well—certainly a lot better than she had done. And, in spite of everything she had told herself about how much easier it would be if she and Torr were friends, what she remembered most about the night was the feel of his mouth on her shoulder.

Mallory shivered slightly at the memory. She wasn't quite sure how that had felt, but it certainly wasn't like being friends.

So she was relieved when she came back from walking Charlie to discover that the kitchen was empty. Torr had tidied up and disappeared to his survey.

Having wrinkled her nose at the state of it when she was getting dressed that morning, Mallory decided to tackle the bedroom first. She found a pair of rubber gloves, pushed up the sleeves of her fleece and pulled the bed into the centre of the room with a determined expression. If she was going to do this, she would do it properly.

When Torr came to find her a few hours later she was on her knees, wiping down the skirting board with a damp cloth. It was always so cold when she was dressing and undressing that she hadn't wasted time inspecting the room properly, and when she did, she was horrified that she had actually spent two nights in it.

She had spent the morning brushing down spiders' webs, sweeping under the bed and vacuuming every inch of the floor. She had emptied out the musty wardrobe, and removed the old newspapers that lined the drawers in the chest. Most of them were dated 1976, and, judging by the accumulated dust and dirt, Mallory wouldn't have been at all surprised to discover that was the last time the room had been cleaned at all.

Now the furniture had been wiped and polished, the window was clean, and she was just about to wash the floor. It was dirty work, and she had soon removed her fleece, so her T-shirt was looking distinctly grubby.

Torr paused in the doorway. 'I've put the kettle on. Do you want some lunch?'

'That sounds great.' Mallory sat back on her heels and wiped the hair from her forehead with the back of her arm, unaware that she was leaving a dusty smear. 'I've just finished.'

Looking around the room, Torr's gaze came back to rest on her face, and one corner of his mouth quirked. The silky dark hair was tied back in a ponytail, but stray strands were sticking to her forehead and there were smudges of dirt on her nose and cheeks. She was almost unrecognisable from the stylish and immaculate interior designer he had first met.

'Quite a transformation,' he said.

She got to her feet and brushed the knees of her jeans. 'It was absolutely disgusting,' she told him.

'Actually, I was thinking about you.'

'Oh.' Mallory laughed awkwardly and grimaced as she looked down at her filthy T-shirt. 'I must look a complete mess!'

'I was just thinking that you look better than I've ever seen you,' said Torr slowly.

There was a tiny pause. Her eyes met his, only to skitter away. 'What, with spiders' webs in my hair, smut on my nose and dirty jeans?'

'Even with all of that.'

'You've done a good job in here,' said Torr that night, as he sat on the edge of the bed to take off his socks. He looked around him. 'It's not a bad room now you can see it properly. It seems twice as big, for a start.'

'I know.' Mallory propped herself up on one elbow to survey the results of her hard work with some satisfaction. She had washed the walls as well as the floor, before packing away their clothes in the newly polished chest of drawers and the rickety old wardrobe, which had had an airing for the first time in years. Even in the feeble light of the overhead bulb the room seemed fresher and cleaner and tidier, and bigger, as Torr had said. It smelt better, too.

'All it needs now is a lick of paint,' she said. 'I thought I would do the bathroom and the kitchen as well. It would make all the difference.'

'Good idea,' said Torr. 'Let's get some paint in Inverness next week.'

Mallory brightened and pulled herself higher on her

pillows, momentarily forgetting the awkwardness of going to bed with him. 'What about a couple of bedside lamps? They would make the room look so much nicer, and it would save you groping your way to bed in the dark.'

'Get whatever you want,' said Torr, hoicking his jumper off by the scruff of its neck. 'In fact, you'd better start a list. We won't be able to go very often, so we'd better make the most of it.'

'If I get whatever I want it's going to be very long list,' said Mallory, to distract herself from fact that Torr was taking off his trousers without the slightest embarrassment.

She was tempted to duck back under the duvet, but it was too late to pretend that she was asleep, and anyway, it seemed a bit silly. It hadn't been an uncomfortable evening. There had been that moment before lunch, when something had flared in the air between them, but then Torr had turned away, talking about sandwiches, and it had gone. Lunch had been easy, and that evening they had cooked a meal together and then shared another warming whisky in front of the fire. Mallory had let herself believe that everything would be all right after all. It hadn't even been that awkward coming to bed tonight, so it would be a shame to spoil the atmosphere now by suddenly turning coy.

'What more could you want when you've got all this?' said Torr, gesturing ironically around the room as he went over to switch off the light.

'It's paradise as it is, I know,' she told him in the same spirit, 'but perhaps just one or two tiny things—a heater, for instance, and a lampshade, a blind, a new mattress, a rug, a chair, a dirty clothes basket, a mirror—would make it even more perfect.'

'If you're thinking of getting all that, we'd better take the trailer!'

The light snapped off and the room was plunged into darkness. Mallory held her breath, waiting for Torr to get into bed beside her, and when she felt the mattress sag she exhaled very slowly. It was all very well, making practical arrangements and talking about being friends, but the physical reality of a man in your bed was hard to ignore.

She cleared her throat. 'It wouldn't take that much to make ourselves more comfortable. An electric blanket—that's another thing,' she remembered, because somehow it seemed easier to talk than to lie there thinking about how close he was, and wondering whether she would be able to press into his warmth again. Would he turn his back to her, like last night?

Torr was making himself comfortable, thumping his pillow into shape. 'What on earth do you want an electric blanket for?'

'Why do you think? It's freezing in here!'

'But you've got me to keep you warm,' Torr pointed out.

There was a shade of reproach in his voice, and Mallory wished that she could see his face. She *thought* he was teasing, but she wasn't quite sure. Not that she could ever tell what he was thinking by looking at him anyway. Torr was inscrutability personified.

Strange to think that before they'd come here it would never have occurred to her that he might be teasing, that a sardonic sense of humour lay behind the austere mask he wore. They had been strangers until now, going through the motions of a marriage, he grim and distant, she wrapped in frozen misery. Less than a week at Kincaillie, and they had both changed.

'If we had an electric blanket I'd be warm enough to stay on my own side of the bed, and I'm sure you'd be a lot more comfortable.'

'I'm sure I would be, too.' There it was again, that under-current of dry amusement. Had it always been there? Mallory wondered. Perhaps she just hadn't been listening for it before. 'Our marriage may not be very exciting or pas-sionate,' he said, 'but at least it could be about keeping each other warm.'

Mallory wasn't entirely sure how she felt about that. Of course she was relieved that Torr had accepted her reluctance to sleep with him so completely, but did that mean he found her unexciting too?

Still, she could hardly start objecting to the lack of passion and excitement between them now. 'We should have made it part of our new agreement,' she said, trying to match his tone, but not really succeeding. She had a nasty feeling she just sounded petulant instead.

'Agreement?' Torr's voice came out of the darkness.

'The one where I stay for a year,' she reminded him a little tartly. How many agreements did they have, after all?

'Oh, that agreement,' said Torr. 'Yes, perhaps we should add a clause. Clause seven (b), subsection (iv): no sex, but entitled to use each other as substitute for hot water bottle. And talking of hot water bottles,' he went on, shifting on his side to face her, 'we may as well get settled now. Come here.'

In spite of herself, Mallory tensed as he reached for her, and all the breath whooshed out of her at the touch of his hands. 'Now you won't need to come creeping up to me like you did last night, will you?' he said in her ear.

'You were asleep!' she protested involuntarily.

'Not all the time.' Torr shifted to make himself comfort-able, and tucked her closer into the curve of his body. 'You can relax now. The terms of our revised agreement are quite clear,' he said in a mock businesslike tone. 'No sex. No passion. No excitement. And no touching other than in the interests of warmth. That's what you want, isn't it?'

'Er...yes,' said Mallory, and then was appalled at how doubtful she sounded. Because that *was* what she had wanted. What she still wanted.

Wasn't it?

'Yes,' she said again more firmly.

'Well, now we both know where we are, we can get comfortable and go to sleep,' said Torr.

If only it were as easy as that! The longer she lay there, the less comfortable Mallory felt. It was all right for Torr, who seemed to be able to fall asleep without any problem, but how could she relax when her mind was still fizzing? When, instead of feeling reassured by Torr's matter-of-fact attitude, she was letting her thoughts start to drift perversely in quite the wrong direction? When she couldn't seem to stop herself wondering what it would be like if they had an exciting, passionate marriage after all?

What would it be like if they could touch each other? If they *did* touch? If they couldn't keep their hands off each other? Mallory screwed her eyes tightly shut in an attempt to blank out the picture that was forming in her mind with alarming clarity, but it was no good. She saw herself turning within Torr's arms so that she could let her hands drift over his flank, under his T-shirt to feel his warm, smooth flesh, down to the bottom of his spine. She saw him smile in response and kiss her throat the way he had kissed her last night, but this time he didn't fall back into sleep. He didn't stop. His mouth was travelling tantalisingly downwards, his lips slow and sure along her clavicle, at her breast...

Startled—no, shocked—by how clearly she could imagine it, Mallory sucked in her breath. Her heart was thudding and deep inside her a long-buried hunger was uncoiling with ter-rifying speed—as if Torr really was kissing her, if his hands really were exploring her possessively.

This was crazy! What was she doing fantasising about *Torr*? She had only just got round to thinking of him as a friend, let alone as a husband, a lover.

Lover. The thought stopped the breath in her throat. She wasn't ready for that. She had never been able to imagine wanting anyone but Steve to touch her, but there was no denying that her hormones were stirring.

It must be the situation, Mallory tried to reassure herself. It was nothing to do with Torr himself, and it didn't mean anything. It was just that it was hard *not* to think about what might happen when a man and woman lay closer together in the dark.

Not that Torr appeared to have any difficulty in putting it out of his mind. What was it he had called her once? *A marble statue.* If he still thought of her like that it was no wonder he had made no effort to persuade her to change her mind.

Which was good, of course, she remembered hurriedly. If Torr wanted her, it would be hard to resist him in this bed. If he rolled her beneath him, if his palm was warm against her leg, if it slid tantalisingly up her calf, gentle behind her knee, smoothing over her thigh. If his lips teased down her throat, if his body was hard and his hands possessive.

And she would want to resist him...wouldn't she?

Mallory's mouth was dry, and she couldn't prevent a slow shiver of something perilously close to anticipation.

'It's not that cold,' Torr tutted through the darkness, but his hold tightened anyway.

Mallory swallowed hard. Cold was the last thing she felt right then!

'It takes me a long time to warm up,' she muttered, which was the best explanation she could come up with when her pulse was booming so distractedly.

'You can say that again,' said Torr, but so quietly that Mallory wasn't sure that she was meant to hear him.

By the time they left for Inverness Mallory's list had grown so long that they did indeed take the trailer. The kitchen and bathroom had both been cleaned beyond recognition, and she was starting to look at them with a designer's eye.

The kitchen especially could be a lovely room, Mallory had realised with pleasure. Cleaning the windows alone had had a startling effect. She had explored some of the rooms upstairs, where she had found a whole stash of curtains that had been folded and put away. Most were damp and dirty, but all some needed was a good wash, and she was glad that she'd brought her sewing machine with her. She planned to adapt a pair for the bedroom, and use the material to make blinds for the kitchen too. Batons and cords were on her list to buy in Inverness.

Once the kitchen and bathroom were ready for painting, Mallory had turned her attention to the kitchen garden. She'd been there with Charlie one day when she had recognised a blackcurrant bush, half strangled by the tangle of under-growth. She had found some straggly rosemary too, and had begun to wonder what other plants had survived the years of neglect.

'This would have been a thriving garden once,' Torr had said. 'Kincaillie was a busy place in its heyday in the nine-teenth century. Judging from the stories my grandfather used to tell, there were lots of servants, and the family used to have house parties and shooting parties. All those people had to be fed, so presumably a lot of the fresh fruit and vegetables were grown here.'

It was hard to imagine Kincaillie alive with people and laughter, Mallory had thought, surveying the tangled garden, but she'd poked around in the outbuildings and found a rusty old fork. Once she had started to clear, she'd found all sorts of fruit bushes and old raspberry canes. Apples and pears were pleached along the south facing wall, and there were great clumps of rhubarb gone to seed.

Having never had more than a pretty little courtyard garden in Ellsborough, Mallory hadn't thought of growing vegetables before, but now she was seized with a most unlikely enthusiasm for it, and had added gardening tools and an instruction book to her list.

Between cleaning and exploring, and walking Charlie and making plans, it was amazing how quickly the fortnight had gone. Astounding, too, how quickly she was getting used to Kincaillie. There was surprising satisfaction to be had in steadily clearing and cleaning their living quarters, and Mallory was positively looking forward to painting the rooms now that she could see their potential.

She was even beginning to contemplate the much bigger task of starting work on the rest of the castle with interest rather than horror. She was finding her way around, and it now seemed quite ordinary to pick her way across weed-infested flagstones, up and down worn stone stairwells and past rusting suits of armour.

Every day she and Charlie explored a little bit further outside, although they stuck to the shore as much as possible. Mallory told herself it was because she didn't want to get lost, and because Charlie was so happy by the sea, but the truth was that the looming mountains still frightened her. They were so big and so bare, and they made her feel very small. She was always glad to get back to the familiar kitchen.

So, while it would be too much to say that she was feeling at home, she was definitely feeling more positive. Perhaps she wouldn't have chosen to spend a year at Kincaillie under normal circumstances, but the prospect was certainly less bleak than it had been when she'd arrived.

Things were much easier with Torr, too. Just as she had hoped, the hard physical work gave her less time to think about Steve, and sometimes it was possible to think that her shattered heart might even be slowly healing. Torr had showed her how to use the range, and they took it in turns to cook in the evening, with Charlie getting under their feet and music in the background. Afterwards they sat by the fire like a staid married couple, and talked easily about everything except the state of their marriage or life before they came to Kincaillie.

It all felt very normal.

The only thing Mallory couldn't get used to was sleeping with Torr. Tired as she was at the end of every day, she was always reluctant to leave the fire for the bedroom. It was more than the cold, though. In spite of their agreement, the more times they shared the bed, the more awkward it felt—or that was how it seemed to Mallory, anyway. Somehow it had been easier when they were hostile to each other.

Torr always offered to take Charlie out for a last run while she got ready for bed, so she was huddled up under the duvet and piles of blankets before he came in. And then the conversation which had been easy by the fire in the kitchen suddenly dried up, and there wasn't quite enough oxygen in the little room.

Mallory tried to get over it by being as matter-of-fact as Torr himself, but she was excruciatingly aware of him every time they settled themselves close together, and it made her so tense that she found it difficult to get to sleep.

At least in Inverness they were likely to get a mattress without a great dip in the middle, she told herself. She was looking forward to the trip with the same excitement with which she had once planned a visit to Paris. It was hard to believe that she'd only been at Kincaillie two weeks. She might be making the best of things here, but she still craved some city air, some noise and some crowds, and some paving stones beneath her feet.

When Torr had studied the list she had drawn up, his brows had crawled up to his hairline as he'd turned the page. 'There's no way we'll get all this in a day—even if we didn't have the architect to see. We'll need to do a big supermarket shop too. We'd better spend the night,' he'd decided.

'What about Charlie?' Mallory had asked.

'We'll take him with us. I'm sure we can find a hotel that accepts dogs.'

Better and better.

Mallory's spirits were high as they set off early that morning. It was the first time she had left Kincaillie since they had arrived in the middle of that awful storm, and excitement tingled along her veins as they hit the tarmac road at the end of the Kincaillie track at last.

She looked about her with interest. The darkness had been so complete when they'd arrived that she had seen none of this before. For a while it was just more hills, but after fifteen miles or so they came to a sizeable village, with a post office-cum-general store and a square whitewashed hotel.

'Civilisation at last!'

Amusement bracketed Torr's mouth. 'This is Carraig,' he said. 'You may mock, but there's more here than you think. This will be the hub of your social life for the next year!'

Mallory eyed the single empty street. It was hard to imagine she would find any kindred spirits here. 'I think I may be popping up to Inverness for a fix of city life instead,' she said, and Torr glanced at her.

'You might change your mind when you find out how long it takes us to get there.'

CHAPTER SIX

AFTER two weeks of isolation, Inverness seemed incredibly busy. Mallory blinked at the traffic. Here were the people, the cars, the shops and all the signs of a thriving city that she had missed so much at Kincaillie, but instead of feeling at home she felt like a stranger arriving in a different country.

Perhaps it was just because she was English?

They checked in at the hotel first. Torr had booked separate rooms without asking her, and Mallory told herself that she was relieved.

'Didn't they think it was a bit odd?' she whispered as they waited for their key. 'A married couple asking for separate rooms?'

Torr only shrugged. 'Who cares what they think?' he said, sounding disconcertingly like the ruthless businessman he had been before Kincaillie. 'We're paying good money for two rooms. That's all that matters.'

'I'm sure they must be wondering about us,' said Mallory uncomfortably.

'Tell them I refuse to sleep in the same room as the dog or something, if it makes you feel better.'

'I could tell them that you snore,' she retorted, rather nettled by his dismissive attitude.

'Tell them what you like.' Torr bent to pick up both over-
night bags as Mallory had Charlie on the lead. 'Tell them the
truth if you want.'

'The truth?'

'That you don't like sleeping with your husband.'

A tinge of colour crept into her cheeks. 'I'm not the one
who booked separate rooms,' she pointed out. 'Perhaps they'll
think you don't like sleeping with *me*!'

Torr looked at her. Her hair was dark and soft and shining,
and her deep brown eyes were bright, animating the lovely
face that had for so long been blank with misery. In her sea-
green jacket and turquoise scarf, she was a slim, vibrant figure
in the old-fashioned lobby.

'I don't think that's very likely,' he said softly, and as
Mallory's gaze met his navy blue ones the air seemed to
thicken around them, muffling the sounds of breakfast being
served in the restaurant, blurring the receptionist and the
tourists checking out, until there was just the two of them,
standing there, looking at each other.

Mallory's throat was dry, her heart thudding. She wanted
to tear her eyes away and step back, but she was trapped by
that deep, dark blue gaze. All she could do was stare back at
him and wonder with some strange, detached part of her mind
why she had never noticed how thick and dark his lashes
were before. Had Torr always had that dark rim around the
iris, those creases at the edge of his eyes?

The blue gaze seemed to be reaching deep inside her, as if
he could see behind her own eyes to where she was torn and
confused about how she felt, to the secret part of her that
wondered, wondered, wondered every night what would
happen if she turned and touched him.

The mere possibility that he might be able to guess was

enough to make Mallory panic, and gave her the strength to jerk her eyes away. She swallowed. 'I'd better take Charlie for a quick walk,' she said unsteadily.

'OK.' Torr checked his watch. 'Let's have breakfast in half an hour. I'll meet you down here then.'

He sounded so normal that Mallory wanted to hit him, and had to turn on her heel and stalk out with Charlie instead. She was outraged that he could have been so unmoved by that meeting of their eyes when she was so shaken, and furious at how wobbly her voice had been. Even her knees felt weak!

She was completely thrown by her reaction to him—to *Torr*. To her husband. It didn't make sense.

Poor Charlie had to trot to keep up with her as she strode along, too wound up to give him time for any really satisfactory sniffs. She wished Torr wasn't so hard to read. When he said that it was unlikely that the hotel staff would imagine that he didn't want her, did that imply that he *did*? But if he did want her, why not say so? More importantly, did she want him to want her?

Mallory just didn't know. She was so used to longing for Steve that she wasn't sure *what* she wanted any more. Until she did, she resolved, she wasn't going to risk making a fool of herself by gazing into Torr's eyes like that any more.

By the time she returned to the hotel and settled Charlie in her room, she had armoured herself with such an air of cool sophistication that no one watching her walk into the restaurant to meet Torr would have guessed that she was ridiculously nervous. Mallory just hoped that Torr wouldn't guess either.

She stood in the doorway and looked around the room for him, and was horrified to discover that the sight of him at a table by the window was enough to tangle her entrails into knots. His dark head was bent over a menu, but, as if sensing her, he looked up and saw her hesitating.

Their eyes met across the room and Mallory's heart promptly lurched into overdrive. Why had it suddenly started *doing* that? After all she had had to say to herself too!

Still, she managed to walk over to him with a creditable show of unconcern, and even summoned a cool smile as she sat down.

'I was just about to order,' said Torr. 'What do you want?'

I want to stop feeling like this, Mallory nearly said. *I want you to go back to being a stranger.* At least when she had been miserable she had known where she was.

'I'll just have some coffee,' she said.

'Have something to eat, too.' Torr handed her the menu. 'We've got a long day ahead, and we might not get a chance for lunch. It depends how long we're with Sheena.'

'Sheena?' Instantly and inexplicably alert at the sound of another woman's name, Mallory looked up sharply from the menu.

'Sheena Irvine, the architect.' Torr signalled for the waitress, and Mallory found herself hoping that she wouldn't respond immediately. She did, of course.

Mallory ordered scrambled eggs and smoked salmon, and let Torr pour her a cup of coffee.

'What's she like, this Sheena?' she asked him, feeling peevish for some reason.

'She's got an excellent reputation,' said Torr. 'Her designs have won a number of awards.'

'Yes, but what's she *like*?' said Mallory with a touch of impatience, and Torr shot her a curious look, as if wondering why it mattered.

It didn't, of course, she told herself, but why didn't he just answer the question?

'She's a very nice woman,' he said eventually, and Mallory

promptly wished she hadn't asked. 'Intelligent, talented, stylish. It turns out that she's a climber, too, and we've done a lot of the same climbs. What else do you want to know?'

'Attractive?'

'Very,' said Torr. 'You'll like her.'

Mallory shook out her napkin with a decided flick. Somehow she doubted that.

She was right. She didn't like Sheena at all, and she was fairly sure the feeling was mutual.

Sheena was unmistakably a Scot. She had beautiful pale skin, and hair that Mallory would have loved to describe as carroty, but was instead a rich, glorious red-gold. She was stylishly dressed, Mallory acknowledged a little grudgingly—Torr had been right about that at least—but she managed to keep a wholesome air about her too. Next to her, Mallory felt like a hothouse flower, and about as out of place.

There were the inevitable few minutes of small talk while they settled themselves and waited for Sheena's secretary to bring coffee. Torr and Sheena were talking about climbing, and, as Mallory rarely climbed more than stairs unless she had to, she had the opportunity to observe them both.

Sheena hadn't been expecting Torr to produce a wife, that much was obvious, and it was equally obvious that she was disappointed. Torr must have kept very quiet about her before, Mallory thought, and she couldn't help feeling miffed. OK, so their relationship wasn't a conventional one, but he could at least have mentioned that he was married.

She could tell that Sheena found Torr attractive. The other woman wasn't exactly batting her eyelashes at him, but she was mirroring his body language, and there was an awful lot of looking into his eyes and touching her mouth.

Of course it *might* be unconscious, Mallory admitted somewhat grudgingly, but she didn't think so.

For the first time she looked at her husband through another woman's eyes. Torr's features were too stern and craggy to be classically handsome, but he was tall and broad and solid. His expression was forbidding, but there was something intriguing about his mouth now she came to think of it. In repose, it was stern, but in the kind of way that had you wondering what he would look like when he smiled, whether it would transform him.

As it did. Mallory remembered how startled she had been the first time she had really noticed his smile. Sheena would undoubtedly have noticed too.

Sheena was chatting vivaciously to Torr about some mountain she had climbed in Morocco, and with absolutely nothing to contribute to the conversation Mallory resumed her covert study. There was an air of assurance about Torr that was not unattractive, she supposed. He was short on the easy charm that Steve had had in spades, and he clearly wasn't a man you would want to cross, but there was something reassuring about him too. Torr might have no aptitude for wild, romantic gestures, but you would want someone like him in a crisis. With Torr by your side you might not feel a million dollars, but you would feel safe.

So, yes, she could see what Sheena saw in him. And she could see what Torr saw in Sheena, too. Mallory was piqued to realise that he was talking more animatedly to the other woman than she had ever seen him. They both seemed to have forgotten that he was married to *her*.

Perhaps it was time to remind them.

When all the coffee and the preliminary chit-chat was over, they all got up to look at the plans spread out on a big table.

Mallory made sure that she stood close to Torr. She leant very obviously against him as they bent to inspect the plans. She patted his shoulder. She let her hand—the one with the wedding ring plainly in view—rest very deliberately on his, and ignored the way he stiffened at her touch, smiling brilliantly at Sheena instead. She even dropped in the occasional 'darling', in case Sheena hadn't got the point.

'What was all that about?' demanded Torr the moment they found themselves on the pavement outside Sheena's office.

Mallory turned up the collar of her jacket against the cold, all innocence. 'All what?'

'You know quite well what,' said Torr curtly, turning to stride off down the street so that Mallory practically had to run to catch up with him. Now she knew how Charlie had felt earlier. 'You can't bear me to touch you, and yet suddenly you can't keep your hands off me! And since when have I been your darling?' he asked with a sardonic look.

'I thought I would just jog your memory, as you'd obviously forgotten that you were married to me.'

'Don't be ridiculous,' he snapped.

'I can't think why you bothered to take me along,' she said a little breathlessly. 'I can't bore on about how many mountains I've climbed, and I haven't spent hours swotting up on Scottish history just to impress you.'

'Frankly, Mallory, I'd be amazed if you ever tried to impress me!' Torr retorted. 'I think you'll find that Sheena researched Kincaillie's history as part of the design process, and I thought the results were very impressive. What did you think? Or were you too busy fretting about Sheena?'

'Actually, I thought the designs were very good, and I wasn't *fretting*,' said Mallory coldly. 'I just objected to being treated as if I wasn't there at all.'

'You could have joined in the conversation instead of glaring at Sheena.'

'I wouldn't have been able to get a word in edgeways.' She wished that he would slow down. Her shoes weren't up to jogging along pavements. 'Why didn't you tell her you were married when you met her before?'

'It was a business meeting. The question never came up.'

'Is Sheena married?'

'She's divorced,' said Torr reluctantly.

'Oh, so *that* came up?' Mallory needled. 'Surprise, surprise! I could have told you that anyway, by the way she was looking at you. I would have thought an architect with her supposedly great reputation would have been a bit more professional!'

Goaded at last, Torr stopped and swung round to face her. 'Don't you think you're being a bit dog in the manger, *darling*?' he asked 'You don't want me yourself, but you don't want Sheena to show any interest in me either.'

'It's a question of courtesy,' said Mallory, standing her ground, and grateful to have a moment to catch her breath. 'It was humiliating for me to sit there while you two drooled over each other. I might as well not have been there at all!'

'Why, Mallory, could it be that you're jealous?'

She gave a dismissive puff of laughter. 'Jealous? Jealous? Of course not! If ginger hair and freckles are your thing, go for it. Just don't take me along and expect me to watch.'

Torr lifted his brows. 'Are you saying that you don't mind if I have an affair?'

The question brought Mallory up short. There was a pause while she tried to work out how to tell him that any affair he embarked on would be over her dead body without admitting that she *was* jealous after all.

'There wouldn't be much point in us being married then, would there?' she replied eventually.

'There's not much point in a wife who won't sleep with me either,' Torr countered, and Mallory flushed.

'Marriage was your idea,' she pointed out. 'You were the one who suggested we include no sex in the terms of our deal.'

Dark blue eyes examined her face, as if searching for something. 'You're right, I did,' he said at last. He started walking again.

'It's a shame you don't like Sheena,' he said, as if the last exchange had never happened, as if he had never suggested that their marriage was pointless. 'She's going to be coming to Kincaillie regularly once the work starts,' he said, glancing indifferently down at Mallory. 'She could have been a friend for you. You're always complaining that you don't have any friends there.'

'I'm not *always complaining*,' said Mallory in a frosty voice. 'And I certainly don't need the kind of friend who's prepared to flirt with another woman's husband, thank you very much. I'll stick with Charlie.'

'Suit yourself.' Torr stopped at a junction and looked up and down the main road, trying to orientate himself. 'Now, we've got a lot to do today, so can we please forget Sheena Irvine for the moment and get on with it? What's first on the list?'

Mallory's feet were agony by the time they got back to hotel late that afternoon. In her time she had been something of a shopaholic, but she had always gone with a friend, and they had built in various stops for coffee and lunch. There were no such frivolities shopping with Torr, who had worked his way relentlessly through the list they had drawn up before they left and never seemed to think it might be nice to take the weight off his feet for a minute or two.

In other ways it was a successful afternoon, as they found almost everything they needed and arranged to pick most of it up the next morning. Mallory felt as if she had walked twenty miles at least around stores and along pavements, and the shoes which had started out the day as perfect for a little shopping in town had ended up as instruments of torture.

Torr frowned as she hobbled into the hotel. 'I'd better take Charlie out for you,' he said brusquely. 'At least *I've* got sensible shoes on.'

Mallory was too grateful for the offer to object to his tone. She took her shoes off as soon as they were inside, and limped beside him down the corridor to her room, where they were greeted by an ecstatic Charlie. He wriggled and writhed with delight, and ran around searching for something to bring Mallory, deciding eventually on one of the towelling mules provided by the hotel.

'Sensible dog,' said Torr austerely, as she took it from him with a grimace. 'You'd have been much better off in those. Even Charlie knows it's stupid to go out for the day in heels!'

As soon as they had gone, Mallory ran herself a deep bath and sank down under the bubbles, also courtesy of the hotel, with a long sigh of relief, grimacing a little as she wiggled her painful feet.

The warm, scented water was blissful, and so comforting that she was still there when Torr brought Charlie back. 'Just a minute!' she called guiltily at his characteristically peremptory knock.

Scrambling out of the bath, she reached for a towel and wrapped it round her, snatching up a smaller one to dab at her wet hair as she hurried to open the door.

'Sorry,' she said breathlessly, and then had to grab at her towel as Charlie leapt at her in excitement. 'Charlie, get down!' She bent to pat him, in the hope of calming him down, but it was difficult when her towels were slipping all over the place.

'Charlie, *down*!' thundered Torr, and Charlie dropped instantly to the floor.

Mallory couldn't help laughing at his surprised expression. Still smiling, she looked up at Torr as she straightened. 'Thank you!' she said.

Torr had been smiling too, but as their eyes met their smiles faded at the same time. It was just like in hotel lobby that morning—only this time she was practically naked, which made it ten times worse. Thanks to Charlie, the towel barely covered her breasts, and although she pulled it up hastily, she was still suddenly intensely aware of every curve of her body, every dip and swell, every nerve-ending tingling beneath Torr's gaze.

Deep inside Mallory something was pulsing insistently, pushing the breath from her lungs. The silence swelled and stretched until it twanged. Water was dripping from her wet hair onto her shoulders, and trickling into her cleavage. Torr's eyes travelled slowly over her bare skin, pink and glowing and still damp from bath, from her forehead down to her toes. Mallory would never have believed that a simple look was enough to make her feel that she had been stroked all over.

'Um…thank you for walking Charlie,' she managed at last, struggling for some semblance of normality.

'No problem.' Torr's eyes dropped to her toes once more. 'You won't want to walk far on those feet,' he said, his voice strained. 'Shall we eat in the restaurant here? It's supposed to be quite good. Why don't you knock on my door when you're ready, and we'll have a drink before dinner?'

'I'll do that,' said Mallory unevenly.

She closed the door and leant back against it, closing her eyes. Her knees felt weak and her pulse was booming in her ears. What was *wrong* with her today? This was *Torr.* He might be her husband, but he had made it clear that he wasn't interested in sleeping with her, and only today had as good as admitted that he found Sheena Irvine more attractive.

She really must pull herself together.

For the first time ever Mallory had to force herself to think about Steve. How strange. After months of dominating her thoughts and dreams, Steve's image had receded to the extent that she had to make herself imagine him.

It wasn't that she had forgotten him, but the picture of him had blurred slightly without her quite realising it, so although she could remember the golden good looks and the winning smile, it was a bit like remembering someone in a film. She couldn't remember how it had felt to be with him. All she could remember was how desolate life had seemed when he had gone.

And now she found herself in Inverness, dressing as carefully for dinner with her husband as for a first date. She even had butterflies in her stomach as she shut Charlie in with a biscuit and knocked on Torr's door.

'Are you ready?' she called.

Torr opened the door. He had obviously showered, and was wearing a jacket and tie, but otherwise there was nothing special about him. He looked exactly as he always did, but for some reason the breath clogged in Mallory's throat and she felt abruptly as naked as she had done wearing only the towel.

There was a moment's silence as they regarded each other. Mallory was wearing loose black silk trousers with a camisole and short jacket in fuchsia pink. Her dark silky hair was loosely twisted back, and she had made up her eyes so that they looked darker and more dramatic than ever, while her lipstick picked up the bright colour of the jacket.

Torr cleared his throat. 'You look…nice.'

'Thank you.' Mallory lifted her arms and cast a self-deprecating look downwards. 'You don't get a chance to wear outfits like this much in the Kincaillie kitchen!'

'No, I suppose not.' He closed the door behind him and tucked the key card into his jacket pocket. 'Shall we go down?'

The silence was constrained as they headed for the stairs. 'Are you comfortable in your room?' Torr asked stiltedly after a moment.

'Very, thank you.'

'I thought you might appreciate a room of your own tonight for a change,' he said. 'I don't think you'll need me to keep you warm, anyway. My room is so stuffy I had to open the window.'

'My room seemed hot, too,' said Mallory, not wanting to admit that the room had seemed too big and a little lonely on her own. 'Maybe we're acclimatising to Kincaillie?'

He glanced at her. 'Maybe we are.'

The hotel was obviously a popular place to eat, and the bar was lively without being over-crowded when they went in. We must look just like them, Mallory thought as Torr went to order their drinks at the bar. Just an ordinary couple in town for the weekend. There were several other couples there, and she watched them from under her lashes. How many of them were sleeping in separate rooms?

They found a table and sat down with their drinks, their conversation so stilted at first that it felt like a first date. Worse, really, as they had no excuse to feel that awkward when they had been married over six months. Mallory was excruciatingly aware of Torr sitting opposite, of his broad shoulders, of the hard line of his jaw, of his fingers curling around his glass. She felt jittery and self-conscious, and her attempts to make conversation kept coming out in a rush and then drying up completely.

All in all, it was a relief when they went in to eat. At least then they had the menu to talk about, but once they had ordered, and Torr had perused the wine list, the silences grew longer again. Mallory even began to wish that they were back in the kitchen at Kincaillie, where they didn't seem to have this problem, and who would ever have imagined she would wish *that*?

'Well,' said Torr at last, sitting back in his chair and studying her across the table. 'Are you enjoying being back in the bright lights?'

Mallory put on a bright smile. 'Oh, yes,' she said, but to be honest she wasn't *that* sure. She had felt too unsettled to enjoy anything much today, and she was fairly certain Torr was responsible for that, not Inverness.

'It's nice to have other people about again.' She looked around the restaurant at the other diners, who seemed to be enjoying themselves in an uncomplicated way, who were talking and laughing and not making stilted conversation with their own husbands and wives.

'I've missed that at Kincaillie,' she said. 'I've always lived in a town, somewhere you can pop down to the shops for a pint of milk, or walk to meet a friend for a drink. You can distract yourself in a city. You can't do that at Kincaillie. You can't get away from yourself.'

She hadn't meant to reveal that much about herself, but somehow the words were out before she could stop them. Letting her gaze slip away from his, she fiddled with her fork.

'Get away from yourself, or from me?' asked Torr.

'From myself, mostly,' she said. 'From feeling as if nothing matters and that every day is just time to be got through before you can go to bed and sleep again.'

'Is that what it's been like for you?' The harshness had faded from his voice and Mallory nodded, grateful for his understanding.

'For a long time I wouldn't admit how much Steve had hurt me,' she told him. 'I'd keep trying to think up excuses for him, some reason to explain why he behaved the way he did, because that was easier than facing up to the fact that he'd used me and betrayed me and abandoned me.'

The hardest thing to accept had been the fact that Steve had probably never really loved her at all.

'It felt as if there was a great tangled knot of barbed wire inside me, and I was all caught up on it,' she tried to explain to Torr. 'If I let myself think about Steve and what he had done, it was like trying to tear myself free. The more I did that, the more it ripped at me, and it hurt so much I couldn't bear it.'

Her voice cracked at the memory, and she drew a breath to steady it. 'So I chose to keep very still instead. If I didn't think, didn't feel, I was still trapped, but at least the barbed wire didn't pull at me.'

Abandoning the fork, she lifted eyes to Torr's with a painful smile. 'I suppose you think I'm a coward?'

'No,' he said. 'We have to deal with these things the best way we can.' He paused. 'I understand now why you seemed so…lifeless in Ellsborough.'

'It was like being dead inside,' Mallory agreed. 'Friends kept telling me I should be angry, but I couldn't. I couldn't really feel anything. At least when I was in Ellsborough I could try and distract myself by going out and trying to do things, but when I got to Kincaillie there was nothing, nobody. There were just those bleak mountains and the sea, and knowing that I didn't belong.'

Torr was watching her face. 'Is that why you cried that day?' he asked, and she sighed at the memory.

'Yes. I realised then that I couldn't avoid facing the fact that Steve didn't love me any longer, and it was just as painful as I thought it would be.'

There was a tiny pause. Torr straightened his cutlery.

'Do you think you'll ever get over him?' he asked abruptly, glancing up at her. 'Steve,' he added, as if there could be anyone else.

Mallory didn't answer immediately. 'Have you ever been in love, Torr?' she replied at last.

It was Torr's turn to look away. 'Yes.'

'How did it end?'

He hesitated. 'To be honest, it never really began,' he said eventually. 'It's what you might call an unrequited passion,' he explained, with a derisive smile.

He was mocking himself, but Mallory could tell that it was more important to him than he was prepared to admit. She wasn't entirely surprised. She had suspected that some heartache lay behind that forbidding exterior.

'Is that why you married me?' she asked him.

For a moment she thought Torr wouldn't answer. He was turning his glass between restless fingers, but after a moment he looked up and met her dark brown gaze very directly. 'Yes,' he admitted.

'Has marrying me meant that you've stopped loving her?'

'No,' he said.

'Do you think you'll ever get over her?'

Torr's smile twisted. 'It would be a lot easier if I could, but, no, I don't think I will. My trouble is that I never give up.'

'So what makes you think I'll be able to get over Steve?'

'Because he's a slimeball who has hurt you and humiliated you?' Torr suggested.

Mallory sighed. 'The trouble is that it's not that easy to stop loving someone, even when you know that you should. You must know that.'

'Yes,' he said after a moment.

She mustered a smile. 'At least we're in the same boat,' she said, and his dark brows contracted.

'What do you mean?'

'We're both in love with someone who doesn't love us back.'

'Yes,' he said in an expressionless voice, 'I suppose we are.'

CHAPTER SEVEN

THE wine waiter was hovering, wanting Torr to taste the wine, pouring it into their glasses with great ceremony and fussing around with their table. He seemed to take a long time about it.

When he was finally satisfied, and had taken himself off, Torr swirled the wine in his glass and stared broodingly down into it.

'I still don't understand how you can love someone who could treat you like that,' he said to Mallory.

'I didn't know what he would do when I fell in love with him,' she pointed out. 'I had no idea that he was capable of dishonesty. Of course I knew Steve had his weaknesses, but he was so handsome, and such fun, and…oh, I was always so happy when I was with him,' she remembered with a sad smile. 'I overlooked his faults because of the way he made me feel. With Steve, everything seemed possible. He had a way of sweeping you along with his ideas. I suppose they weren't always very practical, but he made them sound irresistible.'

'Like all the best con men,' Torr commented austerely.

'Perhaps,' she acknowledged. 'All I know is that when Steve suggested we went into business together, restoring old properties, it seemed to make perfect sense. Steve would do the building work and I would do the interior design. At first we did very well, and if we'd stuck with that everything would have been fine. But it wasn't enough for Steve. He started to get restless.'

'Or greedy?'

'Or greedy,' Mallory agreed evenly. 'He started talking about buying up the old warehouses down by the river and renovating them as luxury apartments. I was doubtful at first—it seemed beyond our scope—but Steve was very persuasive, and before I knew what had happened I believed in that project more than anyone else. It was all going to be so exciting.'

She smiled wistfully, remembering how eagerly she had pored over the plans with Steve. Had he been planning even then to dump her and run off with the money? He must have been.

'You certainly had me convinced when you told me about it,' said Torr.

The memory of how cynically Steve had set her up to persuade Torr to invest in the project still made Mallory wince.

'We didn't have enough start-up capital. The bank lent us some, but Steve said that we needed another investor, and we knew how successful you'd been in your own property businesses. When you asked me to design the interior of your new house, it all seemed to be falling perfectly into place...'

'And it did—for Steve,' Torr added dryly. 'It didn't work so well for the rest of us, though, did it?'

'No,' she said on a sigh.

'Do you know where he is now?'

Mallory shook her head. 'The police found out he'd got a ferry from Dover, but he could be anywhere on the continent.

He'll have a new girlfriend now,' she said a little bitterly. 'Steve's not the kind of man to go without a woman for long.

'Do you know what the worst thing is?' she confessed. 'It's not knowing what he was really thinking all the time we were together. Did he really intend to marry me? Did he care about me at all? Or was he planning his scam all along? I had so many happy memories, and now I don't know which ones to believe or not. How could I not have suspected that something was wrong? I keep telling myself I should have guessed what was going on, and I feel so guilty about all those people like you, who lost money because I was too stupid to see Steve for what he really was.'

'It wasn't your fault,' said Torr. 'Some people are very good at playing a part and then changing roles when it suits them. My ex-wife was like that. I'm not normally a gullible man, but she had me beat. Before we were married I would have sworn that she had the sweetest personality you could ever come across.

'Ha!' He gave a snort of mirthless laughter. 'Lynn took me for everything she could get, and by the time she'd finished with me I couldn't understand how I could ever have been fool enough to believe her. It wasn't even as if I was very young— that might at least have been some excuse. I'd already been round the block a few times and made my first million— which I realised, in retrospect, was all that attracted Lynn to me. *I* was pretty stupid not to have seen that one coming!'

'And yet you married me, knowing that I was marrying you for exactly the same reason,' Mallory pointed out.

'It was different with you. You've never pretended to feel something you don't.'

Did it count if you were pretending not to feel something you *did* feel? Mallory wondered, thinking about how adamantly she had denied feeling jealous of Sheena that morning. Perhaps it was best not to go there, though. This might be the most openly they had ever talked to each other, but she didn't have to confess everything, did she?

'Still, I'm surprised the experience didn't put you off marriage,' she said.

'It's the reason I'm not sentimental about marriage,' Torr said, picking up the bottle and leaning over to top up her glass before the wine waiter could come fussing back. 'Lynn certainly disillusioned me about that. At least I knew you weren't going to pretend that you loved me. A practical arrangement suited me, and it was what you needed too. It's much easier if neither of you has any expectations.'

'Is it?' Mallory said a little sadly.

Torr looked at her with that dark blue gaze that seemed to see so much more than she wanted it to. 'You don't sound sure.'

'It's just…' Avoiding his eyes, she turned the stem of her glass between her hands. 'Don't you ever have regrets?' she asked on an impulse.

'About our marriage? No.'

You could always rely on Torr for an uncompromising answer.

'You don't ever wish that things could be different?' she persisted. 'That you could have married the woman you love and spent your life with her instead of with someone who doesn't love you?'

Something flickered at the back of his eyes and was gone. 'That's just a dream,' he said. 'There's no point in wishing for something you can't have. It's better to deal with what you've got, and we've got each other—for now, at least. Our marriage may not be very romantic, but I think it's successful, don't you?'

'It depends what you mean by successful,' said Mallory doubtfully.

'We're both getting what we want out of it. You're paying off your debts; I've got some practical support. It's not a whirl of romance, I agree, but it's working. As long as we both put something into the marriage, and both get something out, then, yes, I'd say it was a success.'

But we don't sleep together, Mallory wanted to shout. *We don't love each other. How can it be a successful marriage?*

But she didn't. Perhaps, after all, Torr was right, and they had a partnership that gave them both what they needed. Perhaps that was enough.

She could see the waitress approaching with two plates. Sitting back in her chair, she pushed her cutlery back into place and put on a smile she didn't feel. 'Maybe when we're divorced you can find her and tell her how you feel,' she suggested helpfully. 'You might find that you can have your dream after all.'

Torr's eyes were dark and blue as they looked at her across the table. 'Maybe,' he said.

It was dark when they got back to Kincaillie the next evening, just as it had been the night of their arrival, but this time there was no storm to rage around the car. To Mallory the blackness felt less threatening, and the looming castle walls in the headlights less creepy. It would be too much to say that it felt like coming home, but nonetheless she was surprised at how familiar the kitchen seemed, and how pleased she was to get back.

The range had retained some heat, and once Torr had lit a fire everything began to look…not cosy, no, but more welcoming at least. In the bedroom, Mallory plugged in the radiator she had bought, and clicked on the new bedside lamps. In their soft yellow light the improvement was instant. When she had made the curtains and unrolled the new rug, the whole room would look positively inviting.

It would be very different going to bed now.

Although perhaps not *that* different. She would still be going to bed with Torr.

Mallory would rather have stuck pins in her eyes than admit it to him, but she had missed him the night before. The hotel room had been wonderfully warm, but the bed had felt big and empty, and she hadn't been able to get comfortable. The truth, as she had admitted to herself at about three in the morning, was that she had felt lonely on her own.

She'd had Charlie for company, of course, although sometimes rather more than she'd wanted. It had been a treat for him to be able to sleep in the same room as her, and every now and then he'd put his front paws on the bed, whimpered with excitement and tried to lick her face. And if he hadn't been doing that, he'd been snoring loudly, and reminding Mallory just why she usually made him sleep in the kitchen. She loved him dearly, but he wasn't a restful companion at night, it had to be said.

Mallory had thumped her pillow and sighed, wondering if she would ever get a good night's sleep again. She couldn't sleep with Torr, and now it seemed she couldn't sleep without him either.

The bed really did look inviting now, she thought, standing back and admiring the effect of the new lamps. She was weary after the long drive back to Kincaillie, and the thought of snuggling down under the duvet and settling against Torr's hard, warm body was dangerously appealing. The realisation that she was looking forward to sleeping with him again was unsettling, even disturbing, and Mallory did her best to shrug it off. She was just tired, she told herself. She was looking forward to a long sleep, that was all.

'I never thought I would admit it, but I'm shopped out,' she said to Torr as they unpacked the perishables they had bought at their last stop. They had done a major supermarket shop, stocking up on all the basics, and as many fruit and vegetables as they thought would keep fresh for a while, as well as some luxuries, including a ready-made meal that went straight into the range to heat up when they got in.

'Just as well,' said Torr, stacking milk in the old chest freezer. 'If we do many more shops like that we won't be able to afford to have the roof done! We'll have to make do with what we can get in Carraig for a while now.'

'We really need to try and grow as much as we can ourselves. I'm all fired up now I've bought my book on growing vegetables,' Mallory told him. 'I'm going to start digging a patch to plant those seed potatoes I bought tomorrow.'

'I thought you were painting tomorrow?'

'That's true.' She was dying to get going on the bathroom, but if she didn't start planting vegetables soon it would be too late. 'I'll paint in the morning,' she decided, 'and garden in the afternoon.'

Torr raised an eyebrow. 'You don't need to knock yourself out,' he said, and something in his tone made Mallory flush. She was obviously sounding too keen.

'That was what we agreed as part of our new deal,' she reminded him stiffly.

He didn't reply for a moment. 'Ah, yes,' he said at last. 'You're working to repay your debts so you can leave in a year's time with a clear conscience.'

Mallory bit her lip. She hadn't been thinking about leaving, but if she denied it he would start to wonder why she was getting so enthused about planting vegetables she would probably never eat.

And he wouldn't wonder nearly as much as she would.

So she told herself that repaying her debts according to the terms of their deal was all she cared about.

It certainly gave her a good excuse to work really hard for the next few weeks. She had bought paint in Inverness, and cleverly gave each room a character of its own just by careful choice of colour, so the bedroom was warm and restful, the bathroom cool and calm and the kitchen fresh and bright.

Having done much of the preparation in advance, it didn't take her that long to slap on some paint, and she spent the rest of the time in the kitchen garden, where she'd started by clearing that one small patch. Mallory was surprised at how addictive she found it, and she got quite ambitious. She planted potatoes and beans, leeks and purple sprouting broccoli, peas and spinach, and once they were in she kept clearing one patch at a time, marvelling at what she found. There were great clumps of parsley and mint that had gone to seed, coarse rhubarb and chard, and a fine collection of old fruit bushes—blackcurrants, redcurrants, raspberries and gooseberries—that had grown woody.

Every night she would pore over the book she had bought, but the best advice came from Dougal, one of the roofers, who turned out to be a keen gardener. Dougal had a seamed, weathered face, and could obviously hardly bear to see her making mistakes. Every chance he could, he would climb down the scaffolding and stand over her in the garden, sucking his teeth and shaking his head.

'You'll no be getting a decent crop of potatoes now,' he told her. 'You're much too late to be putting them in.' He wagged a stubby finger at her. 'Next year, now, you start in February.'

Mallory listened humbly. Dougal told her how to chit seed potatoes, how to grow carrots from seed, how to prepare soil, and he identified all sorts of plants that she had thought were weeds and had been planning to dig up.

'It's like *Gardeners' Question Time* whenever I come in here,' grumbled Torr one day, watching Dougal return reluctantly to the roof after finishing his mug of tea. 'He spends more time in the garden than he does on the roof!'

Mallory pulled off her gardening gloves and put a hand to the small of her back. 'I don't know what I would have done without him,' she said. 'I can tell he thinks I'm too silly for words, but he's showed me how to do all sorts of useful things. I'm going to start early so I can grow a really good variety next year.'

'Don't put in too much,' Torr said. 'Your year will be up before next summer. There's no point in planting vegetables if you're not going to be here to eat them.'

Without giving Mallory a chance to reply, he walked off, leaving her to stare after him in consternation. They had been getting on so well recently that his blunt reminder was like a slap in the face. It wasn't that she had forgotten that she would be leaving in a year's time, or that she had changed her mind, but she just hadn't been thinking about it. She hadn't been thinking about Steve either. She had just been painting and digging and walking Charlie and not thinking about anything very much. In spite of all her hard work, it had been a strangely restful time.

Now Torr had unsettled her again. She didn't want to think about leaving, not yet. Much better to take each day at a time, Mallory told herself, and let the future take care of itself for now. She would just keep on tending the garden, and helping Torr with the mammoth job of bringing Kincaillie back to life, and she would worry about what she was going to do when the year was up.

Dougal and his fellow roofers drove back to the pub in Carraig every night. It seemed a long drive to do, there and back every day, but when Mallory asked Dougal if they wouldn't rather camp at Kincaillie, he told her they had didn't like to rough it unless they absolutely had to.

Absurdly, she felt almost hurt that the men would drive all the way to Carraig rather than stay at Kincaillie. 'It's not as if it's *that* bad,' she said to Torr when she told him about it as he came into the kitchen at the end of a rare sunny day, having washed and changed.

'You've changed your tune, haven't you?' he said, with a somewhat sardonic glance.

Mallory was stirring a sauce on top of the range. She tapped the wooden spoon on the side of the pan and rested it on the edge.

'You've got to admit that things have improved since we arrived,' she said, turning to lean back against the welcome warmth of the range. It might be May, but even when the sun shone the heat rarely penetrated the thick castle walls.

Torr let his eyes travel slowly round the kitchen, noting as if for the first time how much things had changed. Music played from small speakers, and appetising smells drifted from the pot on the range. Mallory was a bright figure, leaning there in jeans and a scarlet cardigan, her dark hair tumbling to her shoulders and her face vivid.

The walls had been freshly painted in a bold colour. She had made fabric blinds that cut out the blackness outside and made the whole room seem cosier. The armchairs in front of the fire were covered by new brightly coloured throws, and the table between them was scattered with books and magazines. Now that they had a standard light each they could actually read them at night now, while the music played and the fire burned low.

Given what a huge room it was, it had taken surprisingly little for Mallory to change the whole atmosphere.

'You're right,' he said as his eyes returned to hers. 'Things have improved a lot.'

Reaching into the fridge, he poured them both a glass of wine. 'Seriously,' he said as handed one to Mallory, 'it all looks great.'

She took the compliment with a word of thanks. 'Do you really like it?' she asked almost shyly. It was always so hard to know what Torr was really thinking.

'I do. I can't believe the difference you've made.' He looked her straight in the eye. 'Thank you,' he said.

'There's no need to thank me. It's just…'

'Part of the deal. I know,' Torr finished for her. 'Still, you've worked really hard, and now everything is so much more comfortable. I want you to know that I appreciate it.'

Mallory was pleased, but his praise made her feel awkward at the same time. 'You're working just as hard,' she pointed out, thinking of the long hours he spent in the rest of the castle. 'It'll just take longer for you to see any real results.'

'That's for sure,' he said, with a brief, wry smile. 'But it's different for me. I've got an investment in what I'm doing because my future's here.'

'I'm investing in paying my debts,' Mallory reminded him. 'Besides,' she went on, trying to lighten the atmosphere, 'working is the only way to stay warm round here!'

Torr looked at her. 'It's not quite the only way,' he said

slowly, and even though she resisted, letting her gaze skitter desperately round the kitchen, something dragged it back to his until brown eyes and blue eyes locked into place so definitely that she almost expected to hear a click.

There *were* other ways to keep warm, of course there were, but as she stood there staring back at Torr, the only one Mallory could think of was going to bed and making love. What was more, she was convinced that Torr was thinking exactly the same thing. She wasn't sure how she knew, but the air between them was suddenly tight, so tight that her breath shortened. To her dismay, she could picture it all too vividly—falling into bed together, kissing hungrily, hands fumbling for each other. Mallory felt warm just thinking about it.

More than warm, in fact.

If he suggested it, what would she say?

She would say yes.

The realisation made Mallory's heart jerk, and she moistened her lips. 'Like what?' she asked huskily. Invitingly? She couldn't decide whether she wanted Torr to think that or not.

'Dancing, for instance,' he said.

Dancing? Mallory felt as if he had chucked a bucket of water over her. He had been thinking about *dancing* when she… No, don't even go there, she told herself fiercely, but it was too late to stop the flush of mortification staining her cheeks. Good Lord, short of hanging out a neon sign she could hardly have made it more obvious that she had been thinking about something completely different!

'Are you suggesting a tango round the table?' she managed, pleased to hear that her voice sounded almost normal, with just the expected hint of surprise at the idea of Torr dancing at all.

The corner of his mouth flickered in appreciation of the picture. 'No, I'm not really the tango type,' he said. 'I forgot to tell you that when I went in to Carraig yesterday everyone was talking about the ceilidh on Saturday. They made a point of inviting us along.'

'A caylee?' Mallory echoed doubtfully, trying to echo his pronunciation. 'That's Scottish country dancing, isn't it?'

'Music and dancing, yes.' Torr nodded. 'You'll enjoy it. Everyone always does, even if they wouldn't normally be seen dead dancing. It'll be a chance for you to meet some of our neighbours, too.'

'What? In case I ever want to pop round for a cup of sugar or a quick coffee?' said Mallory, who was still feeling edgy after misinterpreting his look so humiliatingly. 'Our nearest neighbours must be at least fifteen miles away—hardly handy for a chat over the fence.'

'It's all relative,' he pointed out. 'You never know, you might make some friends. I said we'd go, anyway.'

So on Saturday evening Mallory had a bath and washed the dirt of the garden out of her hair. Torr had said that it wouldn't be a formal affair, which was just as well as she had left most of her smart evening clothes in storage in Ellsborough, but she wanted to make a bit of an effort.

For the neighbours, she reminded herself.

She found a soft, swirly skirt and a vibrant pink blouse with three-quarter length sleeves, which she cinched at the waist with a wide belt. She would just have to hope that it looked all right. The next time she went to Inverness, she decided, she was going to get a full-length mirror.

As it was, she had to inspect her reflection as best she could in the bathroom mirror. She had dried her hair so that it fell in soft waves to her shoulders, and she was wearing make-up for the first time in ages. She looked just the same, Mallory thought with surprise. She felt so different now from when she had first come to Kincaillie that she had somehow expected it to show in her face.

Perhaps the changes were more visible than she had thought, though. Torr was sitting at the kitchen table, reading a paper while he waited for her, but when Mallory went in he looked almost startled. He got slowly to his feet.

'You've changed,' he said.

'Of course I've changed! I can hardly go dancing in my old gardening clothes!'

'No, I meant…*you've* changed,' he said. He studied her, as if contrasting his pale bride with her stark eyes and withdrawn expression with the vivid woman in front of him. 'You look…better,' he said inadequately.

Mallory thought about what he had said. 'I feel better,' she admitted honestly.

'I suppose that's because you don't feel trapped into our marriage any more.' Torr was folding up the paper, searching for his car keys, not looking at her any more, and his voice was curt and careless.

She watched him with a slight frown. *Was* that why she felt better? It must be. 'I suppose it is,' she said.

They left Charlie in the kitchen, knowing that the moment they'd gone he would be up on one of the chairs and making himself comfortable.

For some reason the atmosphere between them felt strained again as they made their way out to the car.

It was long, clear May evening, windless for once, and the sea gleamed like a sheet of copper. The hills in the distance were a smudgy violet beneath a sky washed with the gold of a slowly setting sun. Mallory stopped with one hand on the car door, caught by the luminous light, noticing the setting as if for the first time.

'It's beautiful,' she said, sounding almost puzzled.

Torr was momentarily forgotten as she gazed at the scene. She had never thought of this landscape as beautiful before. It had always seemed so barren, so intimidating in its savage grandeur, a mighty battlefield between the scarred mountains and the ceaseless wind and sea. But now all was still and a magical hush lay over it, and she could see at last how you might come to love it.

If you were going to stay more than a year.

'Yes,' Torr agreed, but when she turned her head he wasn't looking at the sea or the hills beyond. He was looking at her as she stood with her face lifted to the setting sun.

'You are too,' he said gruffly, opening his door so that his words were almost lost. 'I should have said before.'

Mallory's heart clenched like a fist in her chest. 'Thank you,' she said after a moment, which seemed like a better option than, *Why don't you kiss me if you think I'm beautiful?* A more sensible option, anyway.

He was her husband. He thought she was beautiful. Mallory sat next to Torr, her pulse booming in the dark, enclosed space of the car. She was burningly aware of his hand on the gearstick, of his massive, reassuring presence. The light from the dashboard illuminated his cheekbone, the edge of his mouth, the line of his jaw, and every time her eyes slid sideways to rest on his profile she felt hollow and slightly sick.

He was her husband. She ought to be able to lean across and put a hand on his thigh. They would share a bed when they went home tonight, but she ought to be able to turn to her husband for more than warmth. She ought to be able to press her lips to his throat, to trail her fingers down his stomach, to kiss her way along his jaw and whisper in his ear.

If he thought she was beautiful, he ought to want her to do that, surely?

Mallory swallowed, half terrified by the train of her thoughts. Torr had made it clear enough that he *didn't* want that. *No sex, no passion, no excitement.* That was what he had said. *No touching other than in the interests of warmth.*

But if he really did think she was beautiful…

Mallory was appalled at herself. She seemed to be in the grip of something beyond her control, so that no matter how often she reminded herself that it would be better to keep things the way they were, her imagination would simply sweep all sensible thoughts of the future aside and leave her next to him in the darkness, where nothing mattered but the longing thumping deep inside her and clenching at the base of her spine.

When Torr parked outside the pub in Carraig and switched off the engine, Mallory was almost disorientated. The sharp air helped clear her head at least, and she was able to smile and greet people at the ceilidh even though she was still quivering with awareness. She knew every time Torr smiled or shook hands, every time he so much as turned his head.

He seemed to have met a surprising number of people in the area already, which was puzzling when she remembered how grimly unapproachable he had always seemed in Ellsborough. The Scots seemed to like his austere style, though. Or perhaps, like her, it was him who had changed.

The village hall was very plainly decorated. A buffet was laid out at one end of the room, and uncomfortable-looking chairs were ranged along the walls. Dragging her mind away from Torr for a moment, Mallory did wonder if it was going to be an excruciating evening, but once the musicians started tuning, things began to look up.

The music was impossible to resist, and in spite of herself Mallory's foot started tapping. As the first set started to form, she hoped Torr might ask her to dance, but he was talking to the doctor's wife, and in the end it was the vet who swept her onto the floor.

'I've got no idea what I'm doing,' she warned him, and he grinned at her.

'It doesn't matter. You'll pick it up as we go along.'

Had Torr even noticed that she'd gone? Mallory wondered crossly, and was then even more miffed when she saw him inviting the doctor's wife to dance.

The dancing was great fun. Mallory whooped and swung and tapped her feet along with everyone else, but she was aware of Torr the whole evening. Like her, he had a different partner for every dance, so it wasn't as if she were jealous. It wasn't that kind of dancing, and one of the great things about the ceilidh, she learned, was that you danced with anybody and everybody.

Still, he might have asked her, Mallory couldn't help thinking. She was his wife, after all. Every now and then they would meet in the dance, and their hands would clasp as they passed down the line, or swung each other round, and each time his touch send a jolt of awareness through her. There was a steady thumping building up inside her, and her mouth dried whenever she looked at him.

That was what came of sharing a bed with someone, of starting to *notice* him. Now she was reduced to lusting after her own husband, and was unable to do anything about it, thought Mallory, mortified. Ridiculous.

And yet, *was* it so impossible? They were alone, and

neither of them was involved with anyone else, however much they might want to be. God, they were even married! How much more justification did they need? And surely anything would be better than the charged atmosphere in the bedroom every night, lying there and not touching when all they could think about was how it would feel if they did?

Correction: all *she* could think about. Be honest, now, Mallory told herself. The fact was that she had no idea what Torr was thinking about in bed. He certainly didn't seem to have any trouble dropping off to sleep. Maybe he was quite happy with the way things were. Maybe he didn't want her at all.

But how would she know if she didn't ask?

Mallory twirled and stepped and swung up and down the line, and wondered if she had the courage to face rejection and find out.

She danced all evening, and was hot and tired by the time the tempo changed to slow, to mark the last dance. The music was soft and haunting, and she stepped aside. You couldn't dance to music like this with a stranger.

Suddenly Torr was there, holding out his hand. 'My dance, I think,' he said.

Mallory looked at his hand for a long moment, and then, with a sense of taking an irrevocable step, she put her own in it.

CHAPTER EIGHT

His fingers closed around hers and he swung her without
haste onto the floor before drawing her towards him, his palm
warm against the small of her back. Quivering with tension,
hazy with his closeness, Mallory stared fixedly at his shoulder
and concentrated on not swaying any closer, but it was hard
when the haunting music wove itself around them like twine
and tangled up her senses until every nerve in her body
screamed at her to give in and lean against him, to rest her
face into his throat and press her lips to the pulse beating
below his ear.

Torr's fingers were tight around her hand, his mouth
against her hair. The music swirled round them, cutting them
off from the rest of the room so that there were just the two
of them, moving so slowly together they were barely dancing
at all.

Mallory's heart was thudding, her mouth dry. The other
dancers might have whirled away into a blur, silently circling
the still centre where she danced with Torr, but she was pre-
ternaturally aware of everything else—the shape of the
buttons on his shirt, the roughness of his jaw, the scent of his
skin, the feel of his hand—and she could feel herself dissolv-
ing with desire so strong that it terrified her.

There was a last, long note and the music stopped. Around them, Mallory was vaguely conscious of a spatter of applause, but she was still swaying with Torr and she had begun to hope that he wouldn't let her go after all when he stopped moving, dropped her hand and stepped back, his face utterly expressionless.

'It's time to go,' he said.

They drove home in a silence that jangled and jarred in the close confines of the dark car. Mallory's pulse was booming. Her hand felt as if it were burning, and the small of her back tingled where he had held her.

It's up to you, he had said.

She could ask him if she wanted to…and, oh, she *did* want to! She just didn't know how she was going to find the words or have the courage to say them. *Make love to me.* Heat flooded through her at the mere thought. Could it be that easy? Would she have to explain, or persuade him? And what if he said no?

It wasn't fair, thought Mallory feverishly, shifting restlessly in her seat. She shouldn't have to ask her own husband to make love to her.

They were almost there, she realised in a panic as the car bumped down the rutted and potholed track. She was going to have to decide. Perhaps it would be better not to say anything? She could wait until they were in bed and then make a move. Torr would get the idea without the need for a long discussion.

But what if he said no, or pushed her away? Mallory cringed at the thought. It would be mortifying. Much better to be straight. At least that way she could keep her pride intact, if nothing else.

Kincaillie was illuminated in the headlights as they

bumped to a halt at last. Torr cut the engine and switched off the lights. It was a still night and the silence was absolute, and for a moment neither of them moved or spoke.

Mallory inhaled slowly. It was now or never. 'You know our agreement?' she began, but her throat was so thick that her voice came out humiliatingly high and squeaky.

'The one we've already revised twice?' said Torr, unclipping his seat belt.

'Yes.' His tone was daunting, and she eyed him uncertainly through the darkness.

'You're not proposing to renegotiate now, are you?'

'Well…' Mallory hesitated. 'Just one bit.'

Torr had his hand on the door, but he stopped at that and turned back to her, suddenly intent. 'Which bit?'

'The bit about not touching,' she said awkwardly. 'We agreed our marriage wasn't about sex or passion—'

'Or love,' he reminded her, and she swallowed.

'Or love,' she agreed.

'And which of those did you want to renegotiate?' Torr's voice was characteristically acerbic, and Mallory was very glad that he couldn't see her blushing in the darkness. This was awful, but she had gone too far to stop now.

If she could.

'The first one.'

'Sex?'

'Yes.' She cleared her throat. 'I…er…I was wondering… if…if you'd think about…'

Torr let out a short breath that might have been a suppressed laugh or a snort of derision, and she bridled. Did he think this was easy for her?

'I think you know quite well what I'm trying to ask you,' she finished tartly.

His expression was unreadable in the darkness. 'You want to make love?'

'Yes,' said Mallory again on a breath. There, it was said.

There was a sizzling pause that went on for so long that she lost her nerve after all and rushed into speech. 'I mean, when I say make love, it's not about *love*,' she tried to explain.

'No, indeed,' said Torr dryly.

'We both know our marriage isn't about that,' she reminded him. 'That hasn't changed. We've both been hurt. I know you're still in love with someone else, just like I am, but since it's just the two of us, and we're here on our own, maybe we could give each other some comfort? It would just be a physical thing. Neither of us wants anything more than that, but—'

'OK,' Torr interrupted her.

Thrown, Mallory could just stare at him. 'OK, what?'

'OK, let's go to bed,' he said, already opening his door.

Not *quite* the response she had imagined, it had to be admitted.

'Er…fine.'

Well, what *had* she expected? Mallory asked herself, deflated by Torr's prosaic tone. To be swept into his arms with a passionate declaration of love? She was the one who had said that it would just be a physical thing, so it was stupid to feel so disappointed when he was prepared to treat it exactly the same way.

No, she had what she wanted. A little more enthusiasm than 'OK' might have been nice, but she was hardly in a position to quibble.

Squaring her shoulders, Mallory reached for the handle, but Torr was already there, opening the door, and her heart gave a great leap when she saw that he was standing very close. Now that her eyes had adjusted to the darkness, she could make out the planes of his face and the gleam of his eyes, but his expression was as unreadable as ever.

Very slowly, she swung her legs round and made to jump down, and he put out a hand to help her. Mallory was never sure quite what happened then. One moment she was starting to step down from the car, the next she was in Torr's arms, and his mouth came down on hers, and she shattered in a dazzle of relief.

Torr pressed her against the car until the metal dug into her back, but she didn't care. Why would she care when his kiss was hard and hungry and she could kiss him back at last? Who would have thought that stern mouth would feel so exciting, those lips so warm and sure? Mallory melted into him, gasping with pleasure and the sheer relief of being able to touch him and taste him and feel his hands moving possessively over her.

'I've been wanting to do this all evening,' Torr whispered unevenly against her throat as she arched her head back, her fingers tangled in his hair, and smiled.

'Why didn't you say?'

'I told you I wouldn't touch you,' he reminded her, sliding his hand beneath her shirt and making her quiver as he spread his fingers over her bare skin. 'I'm a man of my word.'

'So you didn't mind renegotiating our deal?' Mallory managed to tease him even though her voice was ragged with desire.

Torr kissed his way back along her jaw to her mouth. 'No,' he said, and smiled against her lips. 'I didn't mind. Let's go inside and discuss the details.'

Mallory's legs were so unsteady that she wasn't at all sure that she would be able to walk at all, but somehow she made it to the kitchen, where the atmosphere was immediately defused by an ecstatic Charlie. He bounced over both of them, delirious with delight at their return, even more exuberant than usual, as if sensing that for once his mistress's attention wasn't entirely on him.

'I'll take him out,' said Torr, resigned.

So Torr took Charlie into the kitchen garden and Mallory went to clean her face and brush her teeth, just as they did every night.

But this night was different. Tonight when Torr came in they would make love. Mallory could feel her body pulsing with anticipation as excitement buzzed beneath her skin. She could still feel the heat of his hands on her, the wicked pleasure of his lips, and she shivered at the memory.

It was amazing to look in the mirror and see that she looked just as normal. Her skin a little pinker, perhaps, her eyes darker and more dilated, but nothing else to indicate that inside she was simmering, shimmering, burning with desire.

If only she had something flimsy and sexy to slip into now, but it had never occurred to her to bring anything like that with her.

It had never occurred to her that she would want to wear anything like that for Torr.

How had it happened? Mallory wondered. When had she started to desire her own husband? Since when had the mere thought of him touching her been enough to stop the breath in her throat?

There was no way she was putting on her long johns tonight, but it was too cold to undress completely, so when Torr came in Mallory was sitting on the side of the bed in a pool of soft yellow light from the bedside lamp, still dressed in her skirt and the silky blouse. Her eyes were huge and dark, and her hair spilled in a cloud to her shoulders.

He stopped at the sight of her, then went to sit next to her, not touching. He didn't even look at her. 'Have you changed your mind?' he asked, and his voice sounded tight.

'No.'

The tension in Torr's shoulders relaxed and he turned to look at her. 'Are you sure?'

'Yes,' said Mallory. 'Do you want me to beg?'

Laughter filled his eyes at last. 'Would you?'

'If you don't kiss me right now, then, yes,' she said.

'I'd better get on with it, then,' said Torr, reaching for her, and she sighed with release as they sank back onto the bed together, and there was no more talking for a very long while.

'I've brought you some tea.'

Mallory stirred and surfaced to see Torr setting a mug down on the bedside table. Drowsily aware of a sense of well-being, she watched him straighten the mug and sit down on the side of the bed, but it wasn't until he looked at her that she remembered just why her body was in the grip of such lazy satisfaction. Instantly, memories from the night before tumbled through her mind in a giddy rush that sent the colour surging into her cheeks, and suddenly, stupidly shy, she made her eyes skitter away from his and flicker frantically around the room, unable to settle on anything. She wanted to look at Torr, but didn't dare.

'I don't usually get tea in bed,' she said, unable to think of anything else to say.

'I don't usually wake up feeling as good as I did this morning,' Torr countered, and Mallory's throat dried.

Unable to resist any longer, she glanced at him, and this time she was trapped by his steady blue gaze, imprisoned by the awareness that tightened around her in the humming silence, until she managed to wrench her eyes away at last and reach for her tea with an unsteady hand.

There was a pause.

'So,' said Torr conversationally, 'how's our new agreement working out for you? Are the new terms satisfactory?'

Startled, she looked at him again, and saw that he was smiling, and all at once the tension drained out of her. Relaxing back against the pillows, she smiled back at him.

'Very much so,' she said.

'That's good.' His smile deepened, and Mallory felt her heart squeeze at the warmth in his eyes. 'I quite like these new terms myself.'

'Only *quite?*'

Torr leant forward until he was very close, then took the mug from her hand with slow deliberation and put it back on bedside table. 'All right,' he conceded. 'I like them a lot.'

'How much?' she asked him, teasing, as she wound her arms around his neck and pulled him down onto pillows with her, and Torr's soft laugh sent a shudder of anticipation down her spine.

'Let me show you,' he said.

It was a very long time before Mallory remembered her tea. 'It's cold.' She pretended to grumble, wrinkling her nose as she took an experimental sip.

'And whose fault is that?' Torr lay back on the pillows, dark blue eyes alight with warmth, almost unrecognisable from the grim-faced man who had married her. Had she changed in the same way? Mallory wondered. She must have done. The Mallory who'd first come to Kincaillie could never have imagined wanting Torr the way she had wanted him last night, the way she had wanted him this morning, the way she wanted him now. The idea of snuggling close to him like this, of talking and teasing, and being able to touch him and make him smile, would have been unthinkable.

And knowing that she could do it now sent a dangerous thrill through her.

'Just checking that the new terms are still satisfactory,' she said demurely as she slid back under the duvet, and a smile twitched at his mouth.

'No more quibbling?'

'Well…quibbling's always fun,' said Mallory, letting her fingers drift down over his stomach.

Torr laughed, but removed her hand firmly. 'We haven't got time to quibble today!'

'I suppose not.' Mallory squinted across him at the bedside clock and heaved a reluctant sigh. 'We should get up,' she said without enthusiasm. 'I wanted to finish clearing the hothouse this morning so I can try growing some tomatoes.'

'It'll wait till tomorrow, won't it?' said Torr. 'The sun's shining,' he went on. 'I think we've earned a day off.'

Mallory was delighted. 'What a lovely idea!' She snuggled closer. The sun might be shining outside, but it took a long time for any heat to penetrate the massive castle walls. 'What shall we do? Or shall we quibble about it?'

'You're a naughty girl.' Torr rolled her beneath him and ran his hand possessively over her hip, dipping to her waist and then curving around her breast, making her arch and shiver. He pressed a kiss to her shoulder, at the junction of her throat, and she sucked in a sharp breath as every nerve in her body jumped at the touch of his lips.

'I was thinking of something rather more active than quibbling,' he whispered into her ear, and Mallory stretched luxuriously beneath him and smiled. She liked this game.

'Like what?' she asked huskily, hoping he meant what she thought he meant.

He didn't.

'Like climbing a mountain,' he said.

Mallory's face fell ludicrously, but once Torr had bullied her out of bed and up onto the hill she had to admit that she was enjoying herself.

It was a bright, blowy day, and the wind chased billowing clouds across the sun so that the hillside was chequered with sunlight and swiftly moving shadows. Mallory had always found the mountains grim and intimidating before, and she had avoided even the lower slopes on her walks with Charlie, but today there was something exhilarating about being so high up, with Torr leading the way and Charlie beside her.

The air was sweet with the smell of heather, and birds called with thin, peeping cries across the hillside. Mallory was almost dizzy with the space and the bright light. There was a kind of energy up there, raw and primitive, and she felt bigger, taller, as if she were expanding with every step upwards.

It was steep walking, and by the time they reached the shoulder of the hill she was hot and puffed, in spite of the wind that had whipped colour into her cheeks, and glad to sit down on a rock for a while. Charlie drank thirstily from the small burn that gurgled busily down the mountainside and flopped, panting, at her feet.

Torr had brought a flask of coffee and some sandwiches, and Mallory ate ravenously. It was only a cheese and chutney sandwich, but right then it was the best thing she had ever tasted.

From her rock she could see Kincaillie, far below, and the sea glittering silver in the sunlight. Beside her, Torr drank his coffee, the wind lifting his hair and his eyes narrowed against the bright light. Mallory looked at his strong, brown hand, curled around the lid of the flask, and the memory of how it had felt against her skin that morning made her feel hollow inside.

He looked somehow right up here in the hills, she decided. There was something insensibly reassuring about his capacity for stillness, about his solidity and his strength and his self-containment. Steve had never been still, she remembered. He'd always been gesticulating or fiddling with a pen or fidgeting. It wasn't that Torr had less energy than Steve. He was focused rather than flamboyant, his power more contained.

'What are you thinking about?' asked Torr, who had been watching her face without Mallory realising.

She turned her head to look at him. 'Steve,' she said after a moment. It was the truth, if not the whole truth.

'Ah.' It was Torr's turn to look at the sea far below. There was a pause. 'Are you having regrets about last night?' The words sounded as if they had been forced out of him.

'No.' Mallory shook her head. 'No, not at all. I had a good time last night.' She hesitated. 'I think we made the right choice, don't you?'

'That rather depends on which choice you mean,' said Torr.

'To make the most of our time together,' she said, puzzled by the ironic undercurrent in his voice. What other choices had they made?

He kept his eyes on the view. 'You mean before you go back to Ellsborough next year?'

'Yes.' Mallory could hear the note of doubt in her own voice. Sitting up here in the clear air, with the hills around her and the sea spread out like a glittering sheet below, her life in Ellsborough seemed very far away.

But of course she still wanted to go back to it. Last night

had been wonderful, but that was because it was simply a healthy physical attraction, uncomplicated by love or need. That was how Mallory wanted it to be, anyway. She had been too hurt by Steve to risk her poor battered heart again any time soon.

'We can enjoy now because we know it's not for ever,' she said, uncomfortably aware that she sounded as if she was trying to convince herself more than Torr.

But what else could they do? Anything might seem possible up here, but she couldn't live up in the hills for ever. It wasn't realistic to think about a future with Torr. Even if she had been able to face lifetime in Kincaillie's ruins, how could she ever be really happy when she knew that he was still in love with someone else?

No, it would never work. Much better to stick to a physical attraction that would run its course and leave it at that.

'We can pretend for a year,' she told Torr, 'but we can't pretend for ever.'

'Pretend what?'

'That there won't always be two people between us. Steve and the woman you love. We can ignore them for a while, but they won't go away. Can you really imagine a future when you're happy without her?'

There was a long pause. Torr sighed and upturned his mug to empty the last of his coffee into the heather. 'No,' he said eventually, without looking at Mallory. 'No, I don't think I can.'

The long walk seemed to have tired Charlie out, and for the next few days he was very quiet. He lost his appetite and was happy just to sleep in the long grass while Mallory carried on digging in the kitchen garden.

'I hope that walk wasn't too far for him,' she fretted to Torr.

'He's always been so bouncy that I forget he isn't a young dog anymore.'

'Why don't you get the vet to check him over?'

Mallory made a face. 'I *could,* but he does hate going to the vet. He's an awful baby about it. If he doesn't get better soon, though, I will.'

Fortunately, the mention of the vet seemed to rejuvenate Charlie miraculously, and the very next day he seemed back to his old self. Mallory took him down to the beach and was reassured to see him bounding into the waves.

'I think he's fine,' she said to Torr that evening, much relieved.

Privately she had wondered if Charlie was jealous that a large part of her attention had shifted to Torr, and she made a point of making an extra fuss of the dog, which made him very happy. When his tail was thumping and his eyes closed in ecstasy as she pulled gently at his ears, it was hard to believe that there was anything wrong with him at all.

The niggling worry about Charlie aside, Mallory was happier than she had been since before Steve left her. They were enjoying a spell of fine, dry weather, and it was impossible for her spirits not to lift when the sky was bright and blue and the air was soft and the sea glittered in the sunlight. The roofers were making progress, and with Dougal's advice she was beginning to see some results in the garden. Mallory would never have believed that the back-breaking work of clearing and digging and planting could be so satisfying.

And then there was Torr.

Sometimes she felt quite dizzy when she looked at him. He might just be up on the scaffolding, talking to the builders, or filling the kettle, or brushing the dust from his hair at the end of the day, but the sight of him would make her heart flip and send the oxygen in a giddy rush to her brain.

And that was nothing compared to how her body reacted when he pulled off his clothes at night and reached for her with a smile. The very thought of that was enough to dry the breath in Mallory's throat and set her senses churning and clenching with desire.

She was in lust with her own husband, Mallory acknowledged to herself. Embarrassingly so, in fact.

At least she wasn't in love with him. That really *would* be embarrassing. Mallory was careful not even to contemplate the possibility. They had been through all this before, in any case. She knew that Torr's heart lay elsewhere, and the thought of falling in love and exposing herself to being hurt again was terrifying. It left her feeling edgy and vulnerable. Don't even *go* there, she warned herself sternly.

So Mallory kept a careful guard on her heart and told herself that she was happy to live day by day.

She was less happy when Torr informed her one evening that Sheena Irvine would be coming down from Inverness to see how the work was progressing.

'We'd better give her a decent lunch,' he said.

Mallory pursed her lips. 'Why can't she have a sandwich like the rest of us?'

'Because she's coming just for a day. It'll be a long drive for her.' Torr looked thoughtful. 'I suppose we *could* clear out a room for her.'

'I'll make lunch,' said Mallory quickly. She didn't want Sheena staying the night! 'I've got to go into Carraig anyway tomorrow, so I'll get something there.'

'Well, see if you can find something a bit more exciting than a sandwich,' he said.

Why was he so determined to make a fuss of Sheena? Mallory wondered sourly. Remembering how blatantly Sheena had flirted with Torr, she had a good mind just to buy a tin of sardines and some sliced bread. On the other hand, perhaps this was a good opportunity to remind Sheena that Torr already had a perfectly good wife. She might not be able to climb a mountain, but she knew how to entertain. That was one of the reasons Torr had married her, after all.

So Mallory made fresh soup and a lemon tart, and she bought bread and cold meats and cheeses at the shop in Carraig, which had a surprisingly good deli section. It wasn't the most exciting lunch in the world, but it looked appetising when it was all spread out on the kitchen table.

Not that Sheena noticed. She was too busy gushing to Torr about what an exciting project Kincaillie was. 'You've done a marvellous job already, Torr. It's going to be wonderful when you've finished with it,' she enthused after he had shown her round. Mallory had been left in the kitchen to get lunch ready.

'I'd love to live somewhere like this.' Sheena sighed wistfully. 'Such history! And those mountains on your doorstep! You could climb every day. It's paradise, isn't it?'

Mallory cut the lemon tart viciously. Why didn't Sheena tie herself up in a ribbon and offer herself to Torr with a label reading 'suitable wife'? And look at Torr, nodding away and smiling, obviously delighted to have found someone who shared his feeling for Kincaillie! Had either of them even noticed that she was there? Perhaps they thought the soup had made itself and the tart had appeared by magic.

It went on like that for hours—Torr and Sheena nose to nose over the plans, while Mallory cleared up around them and wasn't even asked for her opinion. By the time Sheena finally left, she was in a vile temper.

'I think that went very well, don't you?' Torr made the mistake of saying when he came in from waving Sheena off.

'Well, *you* obviously enjoyed it,' said Mallory, who was taking out her feelings on the washing up, banging and crashing plates and glasses together.

Torr's eyes narrowed at her tone. 'I did,' he said evenly. 'Sheena's got some really interesting ideas for what we can do here.'

'Don't you mean for what she can do with you?' Mallory snapped, and he sighed.

'You're not still on that nonsense, are you?'

'It's not nonsense.'

With one part of her mind Mallory could recognise that she was behaving badly. She couldn't really understand why she was so upset. Wasn't she the one who had insisted that she and Torr couldn't have a future together? Torr would be staying at Kincaillie, so she shouldn't blame him for planning for a future that didn't include her.

She shouldn't, but she did.

She didn't want to be jealous, but she was.

Confused, churning with uncertainty, Mallory took out her unease on Torr, who seemed so calm and certain of himself and what he wanted. She knew it wasn't fair, but she couldn't help herself, and knowing that she was being unreasonable just made things worse.

'Sheena spent the entire day simpering at you, and you lapped it up!' she threw at him. 'You couldn't wait to scurry off on your own together.'

Torr's jaw tightened with exasperation. 'You could have come with us. If you'd had any interest in Kincaillie, you would have done.'

'I was busy making the special lunch you ordered, if you remember!'

Hurt more than she wanted to admit by the implication that

she wasn't interested in Kincaillie, Mallory tipped the dirty water out of the washing up bowl with such venom that it slopped all over her front.

'Although I don't know why you bothered,' she went on, muttering under her breath at the mess. 'Sheena wouldn't have cared if we'd given her a bowl of Charlie's food as long as she could sit and make eyes at you!'

Something raw and unpleasant had crept into the atmosphere, and by this time Torr was evidently having trouble keeping his own temper under control.

'Don't you think you're being rather childish, Mallory?'

'If you call it childish to object to Sheena flaunting her qualifications to be the next Lady of Kincaillie in front of my face. *"This is paradise, Torr,"*' Mallory mimicked with an atrocious Scottish accent. '*"I'd so love to live here, Torr. We could go climbing every day. Oh, and by the way, Torr, I'd be so much better a wife for you than Mallory, who's only good for making lemon tart."*'

'Why do you care, anyway?' Torr demanded, losing the battle with his temper at last. 'You're going back to Ellsborough, as you keep saying. It won't be anything to do with you. But now you come to mention it, I think you're right. Sheena would make a perfect Lady of Kincaillie. She wouldn't make a fuss about the conditions here.'

'No, I dare say she wouldn't have wasted a moment's time cleaning the bathroom or getting rid of the spiders' webs in the bedroom, would she?' Mallory practically spat out. 'What a waste of time, when you could have been running up and down mountains together!'

'Well, it's not too late,' said Torr, his mouth a compressed line and a white shade around his mouth. 'I'll invite her down for the weekend when you've gone.'

When you've gone. Funny how three simple words could twist her entrails into a painful knot that made Mallory suck in her breath. How casually Torr had uttered them, as if it didn't matter at all whether she was there or not.

'It won't just be a weekend,' she said bravely, given the fact that she was trying desperately to keep her voice from shaking. 'Once Sheena gets a foot in the door, she'll be here for ever.'

'I can think of worse fates than spending my life with an attractive woman who cares about the same things I do and who actually wants to be with me.'

Torr's eyes were cold and his voice very hard. Mallory felt sick.

'What about the love of your life? The one you were never going to get over?'

'She's not attainable and Sheena is,' he said flatly. 'Perhaps it's time I gave up on that dream. It was never going to come true, anyway.'

'I thought you never gave up?' Mallory couldn't resist goading him, and Torr looked at her for a long moment, his eyes unreadable, before he turned away.

'There's a first time for everything.'

CHAPTER NINE

'I'M TAKING Charlie to the vet.' Mallory found Torr about to climb the scaffolding to the roofers a couple of days later.

Ever since Sheena's visit they had been frigidly polite to each other. Mallory had been huffy all that evening, and when they'd gone to bed she had firmly turned her back to him and pretended to sleep, telling herself she would do something about another room first thing in the morning.

When you've gone. Torr's words circled endlessly round her brain.

She was the one who had suggested that she only stay a year, Mallory kept reminding herself. It had been her idea to earn her divorce. So why did Torr's casual acceptance of the fact that she would be leaving in a matter of months hurt so much?

Mallory couldn't shake the humiliated feeling. She had been happy recently. She had let herself believe that she could live in the present and not worry about the future, and she had let down her guard. She had forgotten the reality of her marriage to Torr.

Torr hadn't forgotten. He hadn't lost sight of the truth. They didn't have a relationship, they had a deal.

That was what she had wanted, wasn't it?

Mallory didn't know any more. All she knew was that the warmth of the last few weeks had evaporated, and they were back to the cold formality of the early months of their marriage.

And that she wanted to weep.

Unable to think of anything else to do, Mallory had gone back to her digging. Charlie lay in his usual place in the grass, but he'd been listless again, and when he'd turned away from his breakfast three days running she started to worry in earnest.

'Do you want me to come with you?' Torr asked now, when she told him about her decision to take the dog to the vet, but she shook her head.

'No. I'm sure it's nothing serious,' she said, refusing to admit to her own fears. 'I just wanted to let you know I was taking the car.'

The stilted politeness was awful. Only a few days ago he would have smiled at her, or taken the opportunity to touch her. He might have run a hand down her arm, or smoothed her breeze-blown hair back into place. She might have leant carelessly against him. Their eyes might have met in unspoken anticipation of the night to come.

Now they barely looked at each other.

They couldn't carry on like this for the rest of the year, Mallory realised. The tension was unbearable. She would have to find a way of sorting it out—but first she had to get Charlie better.

Torr was in the kitchen, about to order materials to be delivered by the builder's merchant, when Mallory and Charlie came back, but after one glance he put the phone down.

'What is it?' he asked sharply.

Mallory's expression was stony, her eyes stark. She put her bag very carefully on the table. 'The vet thinks Charlie has a tumour,' she said, in a voice held so tight it hurt to hear it. 'He says he can feel it. But he might be wrong, mightn't he?'

'What if he isn't?' said Torr carefully. 'Is there anything he can do?'

'No,' she said bleakly. 'Nothing.' She drew a breath and steadied the treacherous wobble that threatened her voice. 'So I'm going to believe that he's wrong, and even if he isn't that doesn't mean Charlie is going to die now. There's no reason to think the worst. He might have a couple of years yet.'

Part of Mallory knew that she was denying Charlie's illness in the same way that she had denied Steve's betrayal, but she couldn't bear to face up to losing her beloved dog. She watched him closely, and told herself and Torr that he seemed better.

Torr never disagreed with her, although it was obvious that Charlie was weaker. He still wagged his tail when a walk was mentioned, but he had lost his bounce and the bright eyes were duller now. Whenever she looked at him, Mallory felt as if there were a cruel iron fist gripping her heart. *Not Charlie,* she prayed. *Please don't let this be real. Make him better, make the vet wrong. Please don't let me lose him.*

For two weeks she clung to the belief that Charlie wasn't really that ill, but he grew steadily weaker until he was sleeping most of the time. When she called him, he would struggle to his feet and come over to shove his nose in her hand, but he was very thin and his back legs were unsteady. Still, he would wag his tail feebly, and the look in his eyes told her that he would try and do whatever she asked of him.

Don't die, Mallory wanted to say to him. *That's all I ask.*

She looked up one day from caressing his head to find Torr watching her. 'He doesn't seem to be in pain, does he?' she asked, pleading for him to agree.

'He's a brave dog' was all he said, deliberately not answering her directly, and Mallory's eyes filled with tears.

'He's dying, isn't he?'

Torr nodded. 'Yes,' he said gently, giving her the honesty she needed then. 'Yes, he is.'

At least Charlie's illness had broken down that awful formality between them. Mallory couldn't even remember now why she had been so upset about Sheena. What did Sheena matter compared to Charlie? Why had she been so angry with Torr?

They hadn't made love since then, but Torr had been there, a strong, steady presence, giving her the space and the quietness she needed, treating her with a gentleness that Mallory wouldn't have known that he was capable of before.

'All you can do for Charlie now is to decide when he's had enough,' he told her quietly.

Mallory looked down at Charlie, who had lain down with his head on her feet, and thought that her heart would break. 'How will I know?'

'You'll know when you'd rather lose him than see him suffer,' said Torr. He hesitated. 'I know what it's like, Mallory. I know how hard it is. When Basher fell ill, my father told me that he was my dog, and that made him my responsibility, so I would have to decide whether to have him put to sleep or not. I was only sixteen.'

Mallory tried to imagine Torr as a boy. He would have been lanky, probably, with features that were too big for a young face. 'That was a hard decision for a boy to make,' she said softly.

'The hardest I've ever made,' he agreed. 'I wanted to keep Basher with me as long as possible, so I kept putting off the decision, but there was a day when I looked at him and realised that I was being selfish. I knew I had to say goodbye.'

He looked back at Mallory. 'That was the worst day of my life,' he told her, 'but I knew I'd done the right thing. I missed him so much I've never had a dog since.'

It was a bright, sunny morning when Mallory opened the door to the garden and called Charlie, as she always did. She would dig a little and keep him company as he lay in his favourite place in the long grass under the apple tree.

She waited for him to get up and sniff the air, the way he always did, but Charlie didn't move from his rug. 'Charlie,' she called, her voice breaking, and his tail thumped feebly at the sound of her voice. Struggling, he managed to lift his head to look at her, but the effort was clearly too much and after a moment he simply laid it back down on the rug.

The claw around Mallory's heart squeezed so hard that for a moment she couldn't breathe. Torr had told her that she would know when the time had come—and sure enough, here it was. Dropping to her knees beside him, she stroked his wiry head.

'You've had enough, haven't you, Charlie?' Her voice was cracked and painfully constricted.

Behind her, Torr dropped a hand on her shoulder. 'I'll ring the vet,' he said.

He drove her to the vet's surgery in Carraig. Mallory sat in the back, with Charlie's head in her lap, and didn't say a word. When they got there, it was Torr who lifted the dog out of the car, carried him into the surgery and explained, but then he stood back so that Mallory could stroke Charlie as he lay on the table. She talked to him brokenly, her voice wobbling up and down, as the vet gently shaved a small patch on his leg, and she stayed there, holding her dog and still murmuring softly, long after Charlie had fallen completely still.

She was hardly aware of Torr talking in low voices with the vet. They went out together, leaving her alone, and it was only afterwards that she realised that he must have paid the bill. At the time, though, all she could think about was the familiar feel of Charlie's soft bristles beneath her hand. He was still warm, and it was impossible to believe that he would never again come rushing to greet her, never bound into the sea, barking with excitement, never again rest his head against her knee and close his eyes ecstatically as she pulled his ears.

Then Torr was there, taking her gently by the elbow. 'It's time to go, Mallory,' he said quietly. 'I'll take Charlie for you.'

Mallory sat in frozen silence as Torr drove her back to Kincaillie. When they got there, Torr went without a word to find a spade, and dug a deep hole in Charlie's favourite patch of the kitchen garden. Very gently, he laid the dog in it, still wrapped in a blanket.

'Wait,' said Mallory suddenly, as Torr began to fill in the hole. Running into the kitchen, she found Charlie's bowl and dropped it into the grave with him. She watched numbly as Torr finished filling in and then manoeuvred a large, flattish stone on top.

When Torr straightened at last, he looked at Mallory, standing rigidly, her face empty of all expression and her dark eyes stark. 'Come on,' he said, thrusting the spade into the earth. 'I'll make you some tea.'

Moving like an automaton, she followed him inside and sat on the edge of one of the armchairs. Unthinkingly, her eyes went to the rug where Charlie always lay, and the grief gripped her so hard she had to bend over to stop from crying out.

Torr hesitated, then put down the kettle he was filling and went over to Mallory instead. Taking her by the hand, he pulled her to her feet so that he could sit down, and then he took her on his lap as if she were a little girl.

'You can cry this time,' he said, as she tensed. 'There's no shame in crying for Charlie.'

For a moment more Mallory resisted, holding herself rigidly, but Torr's arms were safe and strong around her, and all at once something broke inside her and she succumbed to the terrible temptation of letting herself be held while she cried and cried and cried for the dog who had been such a loyal and loving companion for so long.

It was a long time before she was able to speak, but when she could she rested her face into Torr's throat with a juddering sigh. 'Thank you,' she said quietly. 'Thank you for everything you did today.'

'I know how hard it is,' he said, 'but you did the best thing for Charlie.'

Mallory's eyes filled with tears. 'I hope so. I just…I'm going to miss him so much,' she said unsteadily, and Torr tightened his arms around her.

'I'm going to miss him too. He was a great dog. There'll never be another just like him, but one day you will find a dog who'll be just as much a part of your life as Charlie has been.'

'You never did,' said Mallory, remembering what he had told her about the dog he had had as a boy. 'You never found another Basher.'

'I didn't let myself try,' said Torr. 'Maybe that was my mistake.'

They were quiet for a while. Mallory sighed and settled herself more comfortably. Her face was still turned into his neck and she could smell his skin, tantalisingly close to her lips—so close, in fact, that they seemed drawn to his throat by some irresistible force.

Torr stiffened at the whisper-light touch of her mouth, but he didn't pull away, and that tiny, tentative kiss had felt so good that Mallory tried another one, and then another, and another, until she was blizzarding soft kisses up his throat to his ear, and then along his jaw.

'Are you sure you're ready for this?' he asked unevenly.

'I want to forget,' she whispered. 'I want to forget everything. Help me to forget, Torr.'

He turned his head so that they could look deep into each other's eyes. 'Is this what you need?' he asked, and slid one hand behind her head to tangle in her hair and pull her towards him until their lips could meet.

'Yes,' she sighed against his mouth. 'Oh, yes.'

It began very gently, but gradually the soft, sweet kisses became harder, hungrier, more demanding, and their breathing grew ragged. His hands tightened around her and she pressed closer, closer, closer still, wanting to lose herself in the need that consumed her.

Desire was beating in her like a drum, pulsing insistently along her veins and wiping all thought from her mind, until there was nothing but the taste of Torr's mouth, the heat of his hands, the feel of his body. Mallory's fingers fumbled at the buttons of his shirt, pulling it open. She was frantic to touch him, and when she felt his hold slacken she clutched at him and mumbled a protest.

Torr tipped her off his lap, but kept a firm hold of her as he stood up and looked down at her. Her hair was tumbled about her flushed face, and her eyes were dark and dilated with desire. 'Let's go to bed,' he said. 'I think it's what we both need.'

* * *

Afterwards, Mallory lay against Torr's side, her face pressed into his shoulder and her fingers absently stroking the inside of his arm. Torr had fallen asleep.

Sated, still glowing, she let her eyes rest on her husband's face. In sleep, he looked younger, the austerity wiped from his features and the sternness from his mouth. She rarely had a chance to study him like this, Mallory realised with a touch of sadness. They might be physically intimate, but there was still too much unspoken between them, still a distance that made it impossible to look at each other properly when both were awake. Instead, she was reduced to sneaking glances or waiting until Torr was asleep.

So much had changed between them since they'd come to Kincaillie. Then, the sight of his mouth hadn't been enough to catch in her throat. The touch of his hands hadn't tangled her entrails into a knot of longing. She hadn't known him at all. The dour businessman had become the man who loved the freedom of the hills, a man who was honest and thoughtful and compassionate. Look how kind he had been that morning.

Mallory's mind veered quickly away from Charlie. She wasn't ready to think about what life was going to be like without him yet. Better to think about Torr, about the man she had married and the man she knew him to be now. How could she have guessed that behind that stern façade lay warmth and dry humour? He had a capacity for loving that she had never suspected. Whether it was his childhood dog or Kincaillie or the unknown woman who had hold of his heart, his love was unwavering, as strong and steady as he was himself.

Mallory's stroking stilled for a moment as the realisation hit her that she was more than a little in love with him. Quite a bit more than a little, in fact. But this wasn't the blind adoration she had felt for Steve, with the heady rush of passion and the starry-eyed belief that all she needed was to be with him. What she felt for Torr was very different.

Bitter experience had taught Mallory to be clear-sighted about the risk of falling in love, especially with a man who had been very honest about his enduring love for someone else, a man who was deeply committed to a place where Mallory could see no future for herself. It would be very unwise to let her feelings for Torr deepen any more, she knew. She had been badly hurt already by a man who didn't love her the way she loved him, and she couldn't face that kind of pain again.

No, best to leave things as they were. Their physical relationship was more than satisfying, and that would be enough. There was no point in thinking about the future in any case— especially not now, when she would have to face it without Charlie. Mallory's heart twisted at the memory. She had survived Steve's betrayal, but only with Charlie's help. This time she would have to grieve alone.

Beside her, Torr stirred and turned for her instinctively, resting his head on her breast and settling back into sleep with a sigh. Mallory kissed his hair and wrapped her arms round him. Perhaps she wouldn't be quite alone.

She couldn't afford to fall too deeply in love, she warned herself. It would be dangerous to get too dependent on Torr. Their marriage had only ever been a practical arrangement, after all, and starting to think about it as something else would just lead to more heartache. Torr had been open about his feelings for someone else, and even if he were the kind of man to change his mind, which Mallory knew that he wasn't, she thought he would be better off without her in the long run.

She didn't belong at Kincaillie. That was why she had

been so ratty about Sheena Irvine, so jealous of the fact that the other woman would make Torr a much more suitable wife. If anyone could make Torr forget his lost love it would be Sheena, who was so much more suitable for him in every way, Mallory thought dully. She might be married to him, but she was never going to be the right wife for him.

When she went back to Ellsborough, Torr was going to need someone for support and comfort and company. For love. He deserved that, at least. How much better for him to have someone like Sheena, who shared his interests and his enthusiasms. If Mallory cared for Torr at all she should be promoting a relationship that would make life easier for him when she had gone, not being childish and petulant whenever Sheena was around.

Mallory was ashamed of the way she had behaved with Sheena. It was time to start acting like the grown-up she was. She would make it clear to Torr that from now on she would stick to the terms they had agreed. It wasn't fair to keep trying to change things. If she wanted to leave at the end of the year—and how could she not?—she would have to make it as easy as possible on him as well as on herself.

Torr himself had never given any indication that love might have entered the equation. Quite the opposite, in fact. Their marriage wasn't about love, he had reminded her the night of the ceilidh. The heart he kept so closely guarded was given to someone else.

There was no point in fooling herself with the hope that he might change his mind and fall in love with her, Mallory thought, even as she smoothed Torr's tousled hair with a loving hand. That wasn't the kind of man Torr was, and even if he were, even if he *did* come to love her, what would that mean? Did she really want to spend the next few years living in discomfort, far from her friends and her family and any chance of restarting her career?

No, things were better as they were. Mallory felt the weight of Torr's head on her breast and remembered the shattering pleasure of their lovemaking. For now, she told herself, that was enough.

Mallory missed Charlie terribly. He had been part of her life for so long now that she felt somehow unbalanced, and desperately lonely without him. She couldn't stop looking for him, and the slightest glimpse of greyish brown out of the corner of her eye would make her heart leap, only to plummet with the realisation that it was just a rug or a rock.

She threw herself into gardening, in an attempt to wear herself out with sheer hard work, but it wasn't the same without Charlie snuffling happily around beside her. Once or twice she tried going for a walk on her own, but that was unbearable, and eventually she asked Torr if she could help him. He was working his way methodically from room to room, clearing out any furniture, stripping off peeling wallpaper and crumbling plaster and readying the room as far as possible for the electricians, who would come in when the roofers had finished.

'Of course,' said Torr when she suggested it. 'I'd be glad of the help,' he confessed. 'It's not very exciting at this stage, though.'

'I don't mind,' said Mallory.

It wasn't so lonely when he was there, and it was easier to keep the conversation to practicalities. At nights they could lose themselves in each other, but with mornings a hint of constraint would creep back into atmosphere.

It was her fault, Mallory knew. That was what happened

when you had to guard yourself against revealing too much, against falling any deeper in love. The only way she could think of protecting her poor damaged heart was to wrap it up and withdraw as far as possible behind a show of carefully detached composure, but it was a fragile defence in truth.

Again and again, she had to remind herself of all the reasons why it made sense to stick to the deal they had made. The work was hard and dirty, which helped. It was impossible to imagine that they would ever get through it. The longer they laboured just to clear Kincaillie of rubbish and start the restoration with a clean site, the more unrealistic a project it seemed.

And yet once stripped bare it was possible to see each room's potential, and in spite of her strictures about not getting too involved, Mallory couldn't help planning design schemes in her mind. Whenever she caught herself doing that she would remind herself that she would be gone long before the electricians had finished, let alone before they were in any position to start decorating.

'I'm going to Inverness on Friday,' Torr said very casually—too casually?—one evening as they cooked supper together. 'I'm planning a day trip, so I won't have a lot of time, but if you need anything I can get it on my way home.'

Well, that was one way of telling her that he didn't want her to go with him. Mallory inhaled slowly and reminded herself of how cool and adult she had resolved to be. Still, she was allowed to show some interest, surely?

'Are you seeing Sheena?'

'Among other things.' Torr looked wary, and Mallory wasn't surprised after the way she had carried on the last time Sheena's name had come up. Here was her opportunity to show him that she wasn't going to be silly any more.

'Has she revised the plans?' she asked, in what she hoped was a neutral tone—the kind of tone you would use when you were making polite conversation, perhaps, and didn't care at all about what was being discussed—but if anything the suspicion only deepened in Torr's expression.

'I hope so,' he said cautiously.

'I'll be interested to hear what she suggests about the great hall,' Mallory persevered as she chopped tomatoes. 'I thought her idea for a glass atrium was quite innovative,' she went on doggedly. 'A contrast between the very old and very new can be very effective.'

Now she was worried that she sounded *too* interested. Torr might think that she was lobbying for an invitation to go with him.

'You'll have a lot to discuss, anyway,' she rushed on, before he had a chance to speak. 'Why don't you stay the night?'

'That would mean leaving you here on your own,' he said, sounding surprised.

'I don't mind,' she lied, and Torr raised an eyebrow in the way he had that always left Mallory feeling slightly ruffled.

'That's not what you said before,' he pointed out dryly. 'When we first arrived, you flatly refused to consider being here alone.'

Mallory scraped the tomatoes from the board into the pot and avoided his eyes. 'I've changed since then,' she said.

Torr regarded her thoughtfully for a moment. 'Still,' he said, 'I think a day trip will be enough.'

Determinedly cool, Mallory drew up a shopping list and did her best not to let Torr get so much as an inkling of how much she hated the idea of him going off to see Sheena and effectively excluding her from his plans for Kincaillie.

But why should she care? she asked herself. She wouldn't

be here. She would be back in Ellsborough, living in a warm, convenient house, with friends and shops and bars on her doorstep, getting on with a new life.

Torr left early that Friday. 'Are you sure you'll be OK?' he asked, frowning slightly as he drank a quick coffee in lieu of breakfast.

'Of course,' said Mallory brightly. Too brightly.

'You could come with me if you'd rather,' he said, but to Mallory's sensitive ears his offer sounded reluctant, and she put up her chin.

'No, thanks. I've got things I'd like to do here,' she said. 'I'd be glad of some time on my own, to be honest. And it's not as if I'll be on my own for long. Dougal and the other roofers will be here all day.'

'That's true,' said Torr, clearly relieved at the thought. He finished his coffee and put the mug in the sink. 'I'd better get on my way, then.'

But he hesitated at the door and looked back at Mallory. 'Are you *sure* you don't mind?'

'Look, I'm perfectly capable of managing by myself,' snapped Mallory, afraid that if he carried on like that she would end up admitting that she *did* mind and begging him to take her with him. 'I ran a successful business all alone for several years. I don't need you to get me through the day!'

'I'm aware of that,' said Torr evenly. 'But I'll be back tonight in any case.'

'As I said, you can stay the night if you want.' Mallory's carefully cool detachment slipped a little as a trace of pettishness crept into her voice. Hunching a shoulder, she busied herself wiping down the worktop so she didn't have to look at him. '*I* don't care.'

'I'm aware of that too,' he said.

Mallory didn't see him go out, or close the door quietly behind him, but she was aware of the moment he had gone. Something had gone from the air with his presence, a warmth, a reverberation that left a flatness behind it, and for some reason tears pricked behind her eyes.

She blinked them fiercely away. What on earth was she crying for? Torr had only gone to Inverness for the day. It wasn't as if they had just said goodbye for ever.

She hadn't said goodbye at all.

On an impulse, she ran out along the corridor and through the cavernous great hall, but when she burst, panting, through the huge wooden door, the car was already disappearing round the bend in the track, and she couldn't be sure that Torr had seen her wave.

Deflated, Mallory turned back inside. She wished she had said goodbye.

Kincaillie felt very empty all day. She worked off her feelings with a strenuous digging session in the kitchen garden. It was a bright morning, at least, but a strong wind was picking up, and by afternoon it had blown in rafts of rain clouds. The roofers knocked off early.

'Looks like a storm's blowing up,' said Dougal, eying the sky. 'Will you be all right now?'

'I'll be fine,' said Mallory, who had been too busy imagining Torr and Sheena together to care much about the weather. 'Torr will be back later.'

But Torr didn't come back. The wind grew wilder, splattering rain against the windows and thrashing the trees beyond the kitchen garden wall as the hands on the kitchen clock inched round. Mallory made supper, but still he didn't come.

Had he thought she meant it when she said she didn't care if he came home or not? Surely he would have rung, though?

He had said he would be back, and Torr always did what he said he would do.

Heedless of the storm outside, Mallory fretted all evening. Perhaps he had stayed to have dinner with Sheena? But then why not ring? And even if he had left at eight, he should have been back by eleven.

Unless he had decided to spend the night there?

The thought made Mallory go cold. Why hadn't she been nicer to him that morning?

She could ring his mobile, she realised. Neither of their phones worked at Kincaillie, but Torr might have his with him in Inverness. She could call and see where he was. But what if he *was* with Sheena? What would he think if she started chasing him up like a jealous wife?

No, she definitely couldn't ring.

Then she had another, worse, thought. What if Torr had been in an accident? He might not have been able to ring. Oh, God, what if he were lying in hospital right now? Mallory wrung her hands and paced up and down the kitchen. Perhaps she should ring the police?

What could she say, though? I argued with my husband and now he's gone off for the night and hasn't come home, and, yes, he *might* be with another woman.

No, she couldn't ring the police. Not yet.

Round and round Mallory's thoughts churned, feverishly inventing ever more disastrous scenarios, until eventually she had worked herself into such a state that she was ready to risk the humiliation of calling Torr's mobile. Too bad if she woke him up. At least she would know that he was alive.

It was only then that she discovered that the line was dead.

Mallory felt sick. With no phone and no car, how would she find out what had happened to Torr? The roofers wouldn't be back until Monday. He could be lying in hospital, thinking that she didn't care. Or perhaps he was unconscious. What if even now some nurse was desperately trying to get hold of his next of kin? She would rather he was having an affair with Sheena than think of him dead or badly injured.

At three o'clock, for want of anything better to do, she went to bed. But she was too tense to sleep. She lay staring at the ceiling instead, gripped by a fear greater than she had ever known, and wishing desperately that she could rewind time so that she could have told Torr how she felt about him, while a single thought circled endlessly and dully round her brain.

She hadn't even said goodbye.

CHAPTER TEN

THE PHONE was still dead the next morning. Mallory had fallen into a restless doze eventually, but she woke very early, with a sick sense of premonition.

For a few moments she let herself hold onto the hope that Torr had magically arrived when she was asleep. She saw herself walking into the kitchen and finding him slumped in a chair. He would tell her that he hadn't wanted to wake her, that he been very quiet so that she could sleep.

Almost eagerly, Mallory threw back the duvet and hurried into the kitchen, but the room was cold and empty. There was no Torr, no Charlie. Never had she felt more alone.

Panic scrabbled at the edge of her mind, but she made herself stay calm. There was no point in getting hysterical. She had to find out what had happened to him, that was all.

In the bathroom, she splashed water on her face and grimaced at her reflection in the mirror. She looked ghastly. Her face was white and pasty, her hair lank, and there were dark bags under her eyes.

Mallory's whole body was buzzing with tiredness and tension, but that was too bad. Somehow she was going to have to find the energy to walk to Carraig and find a phone. It was a good twenty miles, but not impossible, and she had to do *something*.

So she put on the walking shoes that she hadn't used since Charlie had died, and zipped up her old dog-walking jacket. Some time in the night the gale had subsided, but a stiff wind still blew off the steely-grey sea and heavy clouds jostled over the hilltops. It was hard to believe that it was June already. In Ellsborough she would have expected sunshine at the least, but here she was just glad that it wasn't raining.

Worry and exhaustion had created a tight band behind her eyes, and her head throbbed, but Mallory kept her head down and concentrated on putting one foot in front of the other. She made bargains with herself. If Torr's all right, I'll never complain about anything again.

I won't say a word when I see him, she promised herself. I won't tell him how worried I was. I'll be sweet and under-standing and make him glad that I'm there to take him home. I'll do anything as long as I find him.

On she plodded, with the wind whipping her hair about her face, and dark forebodings circling endlessly and uselessly around her brain. It took her over an hour to get to the end of the Kincaillie track and onto the single-track road that wound through the hills. Surely *someone* would come along and give her a lift now?

But she had walked a good mile or so before a glint in the distance caught her attention. A car was bowling along the road from Carraig, its metalwork flashing as the sun came out from behind a cloud for one brief, dazzling moment before it was swallowed up behind the greyness once more.

Mallory's heart leapt with hope. It was coming from the wrong direction, but that didn't matter. This was the Highlands, not Ellsborough. The driver would stop when he saw her and take her back to Carraig, or at least on to the nearest phone. The road was very narrow, but she went on to the next passing place and stopped to wait impatiently.

It seemed to take a very long time for the car to reach her, and she began to be afraid that it had turned off when the sound of an engine made her straighten and begin waving frantically as it came round the bend.

So convinced was Mallory by then that Torr had been in an accident, that it took a few moments for her to recognise the vehicle that braked hastily at the sight of her.

It stopped right in front of her and the driver wound down the window and leant out. 'Mallory?' said Torr in astonishment. 'What on earth are you doing out here?'

Torr. Torr, with his dark blue eyes and his austere mouth and his dark brows contracted in a frown. Not being cut out of his car, or in a hospital bed, but whole and healthy, making the hills recede with the immediacy of his presence.

He was all right. That was all Mallory could think at first. She stared at him as if hardly daring to believe her eyes, only to find that the dizzying rush of relief was swiftly succeeded by white-hot anger.

'Where have you *been?*' she demanded, the desperate bargains she had made with herself utterly forgotten.

'In Carraig.'

'*Carraig?* Carraig?' She glared at him. 'What were you doing *there?*'

'I spent the night at the pub—' Torr started to explain, before she cut him off.

'Do you mean to tell me that I've wasted all night worrying about you, and all the time you were in *Carraig?*' Mallory was spluttering, practically gibbering with fury. 'I suppose it was too much trouble to drive the last twenty miles!'

Torr drew an exasperated breath. 'It wasn't—'

'Why would you bother, after all?' She ignored him. 'It was just me waiting for you. Just stupid old Mallory, who can't climb mountains and isn't any use for anything. Just your *wife*. What do I matter?'

'I couldn't get through.' Torr had to raise his voice to interrupt her. 'I've been trying to tell you. The storm blew down a couple of trees and the Carraig road was completely blocked, so I went back to the pub inn and spent the night there. I did try to phone you, but the lines were down too. There was nothing I could do.'

'You could have walked,' said Mallory, incandescent at the thought that she had been tossing and turning all night while Torr had been comfortably tucked up in bed at the pub, and no doubt sleeping soundly. He had probably been enjoying a good breakfast too, while she was trudging through the hills in search of him!

Torr stared at her. Her hair was wind-blown, her eyes dark and furious as she glared back at him.

'Walked?' he echoed incredulously. 'You wanted me to walk twenty miles through a storm in the dark, and then back again this morning to collect the car with all your shopping in it? You don't think you're being a touch unreasonable?'

'Unreasonable! I'll give you unreasonable!' Mallory was beside herself by now, beyond thinking clearly. 'You drag me up to the back of beyond to live in a ruin, and then abandon me so that you can spend a little quality time with your precious Sheena! *That's* unreasonable! I've had a hellish night,' she told him, her voice shaking. 'I was stuck in the set of some horror movie on my own, with no phone and no way of getting help, but *I* was prepared to walk twenty miles!'

'What for?'

'To find out what had happened to you, of course! Did it never occur to you that I might be *worried*?'

'Well, no,' said Torr. 'You made it fairly clear yesterday morning that you didn't care whether I stayed away or not.'

'I don't *care*!' shouted Mallory, the fear that she was about to humiliate herself completely by bursting into tears only making her angrier. 'Not about you, anyway. I just needed you to come back with the car so I could leave this godforsaken place!'

There was an unpleasant silence, while the hills around them seemed to ring with her last furious words, then Torr let out an abrupt breath.

'You'd better get in,' he said, reaching across to open the passenger door. 'Unless you want to carry on walking, of course,' he added sarcastically, when Mallory hesitated.

After a moment, Mallory went round the front of the car and climbed in. There was no point in walking to Carraig for the sake of it, and she was too tired to walk back to Kincaillie just to make a point.

It was only when she slumped into her seat that Mallory realised just how tired she was, but she closed her eyes against the tears that threatened. There was no way she was going to start blubbing in front of Torr now.

He glanced at her as he put the car into gear. 'Why are you so angry?' he asked.

Wearily, Mallory opened her eyes, but averted her face. 'I'm angry at this whole stupid situation,' she said as she stared unseeingly at the heather-covered hillsides. 'I never wanted to come to Kincaillie, and we both know that it's only blackmail that keeps me here until I've paid off the money I owe you. In the meantime, I've got to live in a filthy, crumbling dump of a castle and work my guts out doing hard labour to pay off my debts!

'As if that's not enough, you swan off to Inverness and leave me all on my own in a nightmare,' she finished sulkily. 'You wanted to punish me by bringing me up here, didn't you? Well, congratulations, you've succeeded! You couldn't have thought of a better punishment than last night if you'd tried!'

Torr's expression was set. 'I'm sorry,' he said eventually. 'I was late leaving Inverness. My business took longer than I expected, but I should have realised that you would be scared.'

Mallory opened her mouth to tell him that she hadn't been the slightest bit scared, but stopped herself just in time. Torr might wonder why she was complaining so bitterly about his absence if she had been perfectly all right. If she had been less frantic with worry perhaps she might have been more nervous, but as it was she hadn't spared a thought to any imaginary horrors. She had only cared about Torr.

Not that she had any intention of telling him *that*.

'Of course I was scared!' she snapped instead. 'Any normal person would have been! I suppose *you* think it was perfectly reasonable to expect me to spend a night on my own in a creepy castle?'

'No, I don't think that,' said Torr in a level voice. 'I can see that it must have been difficult for you.'

'It's *all* difficult.'

Mallory was cross with him for ducking out of the full-blown argument she was longing to have to relieve her feelings. She didn't want him to be understanding now. She wanted him to be arrogant and disagreeable and annoying, so that she could remember just why she was so angry.

'There's nothing easy about being married to a man you hardly know and then being dragged off to the wilds of

Scotland to live in three grotty rooms with no friends around, nowhere to go and nothing to do, just work and look at the rain and hide from the midges! I wish I could just go back to Ellsborough and be normal again!'

Torr kept his eyes on the road ahead, but as she finished he let out a strange little sigh. 'All right,' he said. 'I'll take you back to Inverness this afternoon, and you can get a train home.'

'What?' Mallory swivelled round to face him blankly.

'If you want to go, go,' he said. 'You're right. It was un-reasonable to expect you to cope with the conditions at Kincaillie, so let's call it a day. Our marriage was a mistake from the start. There's no point in carrying on any longer.'

For a long, long beat of silence Mallory couldn't speak. Torr's calm announcement had been like a fist driving into her belly, and she was still reeling with the shock of it. Had she heard him right?

'What about the money I owe you?'

'You've worked hard,' he said. 'We'll call it quits. You don't have Charlie any more, so you can go and stay with your sister and make a fresh start, if that's what you want.'

He seemed serious. Mallory turned back to stare through the windscreen, thrown into utter confusion by being suddenly granted the one thing she had wanted for so long.

'Is it what *you* want?' she asked.

Torr changed down to round a sharp bend. 'Yes,' he said, in a voice empty of all expression. 'I think it will be better for both of us if you go.'

'Well...fine.' Mallory was feeling cold and rather sick. She had just been released from nine months of labouring. She ought to be feeling relieved, but she struggled to inject some enthusiasm into her voice. 'Great.'

They drove the rest of the way in a silence that reverberated with unspoken words. He wanted her to go. That was all Mallory could think. He wanted her to go, and she had no excuse to stay.

Torr parked the car exactly where he had done the night they'd first arrived at Kincaillie and switched off the engine. They both stared through the windscreen at the great door without speaking or moving, while the silence yawned around them.

'What now?' asked Mallory at last. Her voice sounded thin and reedy.

'Why don't you go and pack?'

'Now?'

'If I'm going to take you to Inverness I'd rather do it straight away,' he said. He reached for the door handle. 'I'll stretch my legs on the beach while you get your things together. I know you haven't got much.'

It was true. There wasn't much. Mallory found the one case that she had brought with her and began emptying the drawers that she had cleaned out so carefully when she'd first arrived. Her hands moved steadily, but inside she was shaking. How had this happened? One minute she'd been promising anything if only she could see Torr alive, the next she had been in the middle of a furious argument.

And now he wanted her to go.

Like a zombie, Mallory went over to the wardrobe and pulled out the skirt that she had worn to the ceilidh. Sitting down on the edge of the bed, she smoothed the skirt over her lap, remembering how it had felt swirling around her legs as she danced, how it had rucked up under Torr's hands when he kissed her, how it had slithered to the floor as he undressed her.

That had been the first time they had made love. Her heart squeezed at the memory.

She would never touch Torr again. Not like that. She would never feel his mouth and his hands and the hard possession of his body, never wake in this bed with him warm and strong and safe beside her. If she closed her eyes she could picture him exactly. She knew every angle of his face, every line at the edges of his eyes. She knew how he frowned, how the stern mouth relaxed so unexpectedly into a smile, the way he brushed the dust from his clothes at the end of the day.

Mallory looked out of the window. She could see the apple tree where he had buried Charlie for her. The kitchen garden was flourishing. She had cleared and dug and planted, and still there was so much to do, but she was proud of it. It was her garden now. She'd had plans for more vegetables, and had thought it would be nice to plant some flowers next year too. But she wouldn't be here.

She would be home at last.

But when she closed her eyes and thought about home she saw the kitchen, with its range and its worn table, and the shabby armchairs where she and Torr sat in front of the fire. She saw Kincaillie, settled squarely in the shelter of the mountains. She saw the sea and the islands, a hazy blue on the horizon. She heard the birds wheeling and crying on the breeze, and smelt the air, freshly rinsed by the rain.

This was home.

Slowly, Mallory laid the skirt on the bed and got to her feet.

Torr turned as her feet crunched on the shingle behind him. His face was set, but his voice was quite steady. 'Ready?'

'No.' Mallory shook her head and he frowned.

'What's the problem?'

'I don't want to go,' she said simply.

Torr stilled. They looked at each other in silence, the breeze lifting their hair and flicking white caps on the waves. Mallory could feel the sting of salt on her cheeks.

'I thought you wanted to go back to Ellsborough,' he said at last.

'I thought I did too,' she said. 'It wasn't until you said that I could go that I realised I didn't want that at all.'

She turned to look out at the islands in the distance. 'It's true that there are lots of things I've missed about Ellsborough, and I may go on missing them, but if I go back there I will miss Kincaillie more. There'll be no garden in Ellsborough, no sea, no mountains.' She paused. 'No you.'

There was a shattering silence.

'Mallory—' Torr began hoarsely, but she held up a hand to stop him.

'I know what you're going to say,' she said.

'Do you?'

'Of course. We've talked about this before, and you've always been straight with me. You're going to remind me that our deal was never about love. I know that. I know you're in love with someone else, and because you're the kind of man you are I know that you won't stop loving her.'

'No,' said Torr with a strange, twisted smile. 'I won't.'

Mallory's heart dipped, but she kept her chin up. 'I'm not asking you to love me back, Torr. I just want to stay here with you and take whatever you have to give. I know it won't be everything, but don't make me go away. I couldn't bear it.' Her voice cracked. 'I can't bear the thought of being without you now.'

'Isn't that what you thought about Steve?' He broke off as a spasm crossed her face. 'Sorry,' he said. 'That wasn't fair.'

'No, it was fair,' Mallory insisted. 'You've seen me utterly wretched about Steve, and I'm not going to pretend I didn't love him. I did, I loved him terribly, and when he left me I didn't think I'd survive. But I did, and I've learnt that it is possible to love again. I don't love you the way I loved Steve,' she told him. 'I was dazzled by Steve, swept off my feet by him. When I was with him it was like being in a perfect dream…and I learnt the hard way that a dream was all it was. It wasn't real at all. But with you…'

Mallory gazed out to sea, trying to find the words to explain. 'With you it's different. Maybe you won't believe me, but the way I love you is stronger, truer. I don't think you're perfect, the way I thought Steve was perfect.'

'Thanks!' Torr interjected a little wryly.

'Well, you're not easy,' she pointed out. 'But when I'm with you I feel safe and…and *complete* in a way I can't explain.' She paused. 'Kincaillie isn't perfect either. It isn't romantic. It isn't a dream. It's cold and uncomfortable and isolated, and living here is hard work, and for a long time I thought I hated it, but when I went to pack just now I realised that I don't hate it here all. I love it.'

She turned back to face him. 'I don't know how or when it happened, but Kincaillie is a part of me now—just as *you're* a part of me, Torr.'

His expression was indecipherable, and apprehension tickled the base of her spine. What if he insisted that he wanted her to leave? She swallowed and straightened her shoulders.

'I can accept that you don't love me,' she told him. 'I'm just asking you to let me stay so that we can go on as we have been doing. I know I'm not the one you really want, but if you're never going to be in a position to marry her…?' She trailed off hopefully.

'The thing is, she's already married,' Torr confided.

'I see…and there's no question of divorce?'

'No.'

'Well, then…why not have me as second best?' asked Mallory, a hint of desperation in her voice.

Torr only shook his head slowly. 'No,' he said. 'I'm not a man who settles for second best.'

'Oh.' Mallory turned back to stare blindly at the sea, her throat tight with disappointment and her eyes blurry with tears. She blinked them furiously away. 'Oh. I see.'

'Mallory…' Torr took her hands and pulled her back round towards him, but she kept her face averted, not wanting him to see the humiliating tears that were trickling out of the corner of her eyes in spite of her best efforts to hold them back. 'Mallory, look at me.'

Forcing her reluctant gaze to his at last, he looked down at her. 'Don't you want to know about the woman I love?'

As if she would want her nose rubbed in it! 'I'd rather not,' said Mallory stiffly.

'Even if I tell you that she's married to me?'

'To you?' She stared back into his eyes, confused. Surely he wasn't trying to tell her that their marriage was bigamous? 'I don't understand.'

'It's very simple,' said Torr. 'I'm in love with my wife, and have been ever since I laid eyes on her.'

'But *I'm*—' Mallory began, still puzzled, then stopped abruptly, as if finding herself teetering on the edge of a precipice.

Torr smiled down at her, a smile that made her heart crack, and his fingers tightened around hers. '*You're* my wife,' he agreed.

Deep inside her something unlocked, and a terrifying hope crept through her. 'Me?' she almost whispered.

'Of course it's you,' he said. 'It's only ever been you. How could you ever be second best?'

'You're in love with *me*?' Mallory couldn't quite take it in. Or perhaps she didn't dare to believe what she was hearing— didn't dare to trust that this wasn't a cruel joke when Torr's laugh would be all it took to send her toppling into the abyss.

'Yes,' said Torr, and took her firmly in his arms to convince her, with a kiss that sent her tumbling over the edge anyway— but instead of plummeting into despair, her heart took wings and soared into dazzling light.

Mallory clung to him, terrified of discovering that this was just a wonderful dream, kissing him while she could, before she woke to cold reality.

But his mouth tasted like Torr's, and his lips were as slow and sure and wickedly exciting as Torr's, and when she pressed into him he was so warm and solid and he felt so right that she knew that it really was Torr, kissing her because he loved her. And, oh, it was so wonderful to be able to kiss him and kiss him and kiss him again, to feel his arms closing hard around her, holding her so tight she was giddy with the joy of it.

When they broke for breath at last, she buried her face in his throat, and Torr laid his cheek against her hair and told her he loved her again, and Mallory finally let herself believe that it *was* real. She was in Torr's arms, and there she could stay.

She pulled back slightly to look up into his face. 'I love you,' she told him shakily, and this time the tears that trembled on the end of her lashes were tears of happiness.

'And I love you,' he said. 'I've always loved you, Mallory. I always will.'

Mallory's eyes were shining as she smiled and kissed him again. 'Why didn't you tell me?' she asked as they sat down on the shingle, careless of the stones and the cool breeze.

'Because I knew that you were in love with Steve.' Torr settled himself more comfortably and pulled her close into his side. 'I'll never forget when I first met you.'

'I came to the house to talk to you about a design scheme for your interior,' she remembered, snuggling into him. 'I thought you were very stern!'

'I was. I wasn't the kind of man who fell hopelessly in love at all. My first marriage was a disaster, and none of the other women I'd known had made me think that anything more than a brief, physical relationship was worth the hassle. I had money, I had sex. Why would I need love?

'And then you walked into the house that day,' said Torr, 'and everything changed. I couldn't take my eyes off you. You were throwing open fabric books and showing me wallpaper samples, and your face was alight with enthusiasm. You were so vivid, so beautiful,' he remembered, stroking the breeze-blown hair from her face, his voice deeper and warmer than Mallory had ever heard it.

'You made the house come alive, and when you left everything seemed cold and flat. I wanted you the way I'd never wanted anyone before.'

'I had no idea.' She put her hand on his thigh, and the realisation that now she could touch him wherever and whenever she wanted made her shiver with delicious anticipation.

'Why should you? You were too wrapped up in Steve to notice me. It was obvious that I was just another client to you, and I told myself there was no point in pursuing you. You weren't available, so I tried to put you out of my mind, but I couldn't stop thinking about you. I only invested in Steve's wretched company because it gave me an excuse to see you,' he confessed.

Mallory made a face. 'And lost a fortune as a result!'

'It was worth it,' said Torr. 'I got you instead.'

'But I was so…'

'Unhappy?' He nodded. 'I know. I could tell that you were broken by Steve's betrayal, and I'm not proud of the way I used your debts as a lever. I stopped short of outright blackmail, but I could see that you had very few options, and selfishly I saw it as a chance for me. I'd always thought of myself as someone who got what he wanted, and I wanted you.

'It seemed simple then,' Torr told her. 'I told myself that it was just desire I felt for you. I thought it would be enough just to have you, but of course it wasn't. Our wedding night…I'll never forget the repulsion in your face.'

'I'm so sorry,' said Mallory, wincing at the memory. If only she had known then how much she would come to love him!

Torr lifted her hand to his lips and pressed a warm kiss into her palm. 'I'm the one who should apologise to you,' he said. 'I effectively blackmailed you into marrying me and then forced myself on you. I'm not surprised you were revolted, but at the time I was furious—with you for still loving Steve after the way he'd treated you, but most of all with myself.'

'With *yourself?* Why?'

'Because I'd been a fool. I'd known how you felt about Steve, but I'd let myself believe that somehow you would miraculously fall in love with me. I'd wanted you to be someone you weren't,' said Torr, remembering. 'I had this fantasy about you, and then I didn't like it when I realised that you weren't a fantasy, you were a real person, and you were deeply unhappy married to me. It seemed pretty clear that I was going to be unhappy too, and it was all my own fault.

'I should have ended the marriage there and then,' he said,

'but I've never been good at admitting that I was wrong. I couldn't bring myself to tell you that I knew I'd made a terrible mistake.'

'I'm glad you didn't,' said Mallory. 'I would never have come to Kincaillie if you'd done that. I would never have fallen in love with you.' The thought made her shudder, and she kissed him with relief.

'That's true,' Torr agreed, winding his fingers in her dark hair and kissing her back. 'But it's no excuse for treating you the way I did. I was so angry and disappointed and jealous of Steve, and I took it all out on you.'

'So you *were* trying to punish me when you brought me to Kincaillie?' She had been right about that, anyway.

'Partly,' he admitted. 'But I really wanted just to see you here, too. Even if I couldn't make the marriage work, I thought I would at least have memories of you here to keep me going. At the same time, I was hoping that a fresh start might help us make a go of it after all— I wasn't thinking very logically at the time!'

'It's good to know that you're not always cool and rational,' Mallory teased him, and he snorted with laughter.

'Cool is the last thing I've been since we got here! How could I be cool when I had to share a bed with you? You were so gorgeous, even in those long john things you used to wear. I'd lie there and feel how soft and warm you were, and I'd smell your perfume and my head would reel… You have no idea what those nights cost me!'

Mallory laughed. 'They were just as bad for me, you know. I wish I'd known how you felt,' she sighed, thinking of all those wasted sleepless nights.

'I couldn't tell you. I was afraid of spoiling things just when they seemed to be getting better. I didn't want a repetition of our wedding night! Besides,' he said, 'I'd promised you that I wouldn't touch you, so I couldn't go back on that—especially when you kept telling me how much you still loved Steve.

'I knew I wasn't being fair to you. I'd trapped you into marriage and brought you somewhere you hated. I hadn't realised quite how bad the conditions were until we got here,' Torr admitted guiltily.

'Oh, it's not so bad,' said Mallory, resting her head against his shoulder and forgetting everything she had flung at him in her fury on the road to Carraig.

'You say that now!' Torr tweaked her nose. 'That wasn't what you said at the time, and you were right. You coped so much better than I thought you would, too, and that just made me feel worse.

'I think that's when I started to fall in love with you properly,' he said. 'Until then, I'd just seen you as a beautiful, desirable woman, but when we got here, and you got stuck into cleaning and painting, I fell in love with you as a person too. The more I got to know you, the more I loved you—and the more I realised just how selfish I was being. I wouldn't have blamed you at all if you'd simply walked out—or driven out, maybe—so when you offered to stay for a year I knew that I was lucky that you were prepared to do that.'

'I thought you were relieved that I'd decided to go!'

'I did feel relieved,' Torr confessed, 'but only because I thought a year would give me a chance to persuade you to change your mind.'

'You didn't do much persuading,' Mallory teased him. 'I practically had to beg you to make love to me!'

'I had to be sure you wanted it as much as I did,' he said, and she smiled at him.

'Are you sure now?'

'Well, now you come to mention it, I might need a little convincing…' said Torr, a laugh in his voice as he drew her down onto the shingle for a long, long kiss. 'It's just as well these stones are so uncomfortable,' he murmured a little breathlessly into her ear at last, and Mallory laughed, not really caring about the discomfort as long as she was with him.

When Torr pulled her back to a sitting position, she leant blissfully against him once more. 'I don't understand why you didn't tell me how you felt once we were sleeping together,' she said.

'You made such a point about it being just a physical relationship that I thought it would be easier for you if I pretended that was all it was for me too,' he said. 'I wasn't at all sure how you felt. Sometimes I let myself hope that you were starting to feel something for me, but at others it seemed that you disliked me as much as ever.

'Then Charlie died, and I hated seeing you suffer again.' His arm tightened comfortingly around her. 'I could see how lonely you were without him, and how much you missed having a dog. I knew you would never be able to replace Charlie, but I hoped that if I found you a new puppy it would be a distraction for you.'

Mallory straightened in the circle of his arm. 'A puppy?'

He paused and tucked a strand of hair tenderly behind her ear. 'That's what I was doing in Inverness yesterday. Sheena told me that she knew of a litter of puppies, and I wanted to see if they were suitable before I offered to take you up to choose one.'

'Oh.' Mallory bit her lip guiltily, remembering how jealous she had been about his trip to Inverness. 'Why didn't you tell me?'

'I should have done, but I wanted it to be a surprise. More fool me,' said Torr dryly. 'By the time I left, I was wishing I'd never thought of it. You were so cool that I was beginning to think that I should just give up. And then when I met you on the road this morning, I realised that it was time to stop hoping. When I thought about the terrible night you must have had, I knew it wouldn't be fair to make you stay any longer when all you wanted was to go back to Ellsborough. I just had to face the fact that I would lose you.'

His jaw worked at the memory. 'That drive back this morning was the worst of my life. I couldn't bear the thought of going inside with you, of sitting there in the kitchen, knowing that you were packing, and that when you came out you would be leaving me on my own for ever. I came down here and tried to imagine Kincaillie without you, but all I could see was an empty ruin and an empty future.'

Torr laid his palm against Mallory's cheek and traced the outline of her mouth tenderly with his thumb. 'I knew then that I wouldn't be able to bear Kincaillie if you weren't here. I'd decided that I would follow you back to Ellsborough and start again there, try and build a proper relationship from scratch if I could persuade you to give me another chance. We can still do that, if that's what you want,' he said, but Mallory shook her head.

'No,' she said. 'This is where I belong now. It's where we both belong. I didn't realise how much I loved it here until I had to face the thought of leaving. Last night was awful—but not because Kincaillie is isolated or scary. It was because I was afraid I might never see you again and I'd never had a chance to tell you how much I loved you.'

A smile that left her dizzy with happiness started in Torr's eyes and spread over his face. 'Tell me now,' he said.

'Take me back to bed and I will,' said Mallory, and Torr hauled her to her feet and helped her up onto the springy turf above the beach. The hills rolled into a blue haze in the distance, and behind them the sea glittered in a burst of sunshine as she headed back to Kincaillie with her husband, to the warm, wide bed and the future they would share, together.

MILLS & BOON®
Pure reading pleasure

MAY 2008 HARDBACK TITLES

ROMANCE

Title	ISBN
Bought for Revenge, Bedded for Pleasure *Emma Darcy*	978 0 263 20286 1
Forbidden: The Billionaire's Virgin Princess *Lucy Monroe*	978 0 263 20287 8
The Greek Tycoon's Convenient Wife *Sharon Kendrick*	978 0 263 20288 5
The Marciano Love-Child *Melanie Milburne*	978 0 263 20289 2
The Millionaire's Rebellious Mistress *Catherine George*	978 0 263 20290 8
The Mediterranean Billionaire's Blackmail Bargain *Abby Green*	978 0 263 20291 5
Mistress Against Her Will *Lee Wilkinson*	978 0 263 20292 2
Her Ruthless Italian Boss *Christina Hollis*	978 0 263 20293 9
Parents in Training *Barbara McMahon*	978 0 263 20294 6
Newlyweds of Convenience *Jessica Hart*	978 0 263 20295 3
The Desert Prince's Proposal *Nicola Marsh*	978 0 263 20296 0
Adopted: Outback Baby *Barbara Hannay*	978 0 263 20297 7
Winning the Single Mum's Heart *Linda Goodnight*	978 0 263 20298 4
Boardroom Bride and Groom *Shirley Jump*	978 0 263 20299 1
Proposing to the Children's Doctor *Joanna Neil*	978 0 263 20300 4
Emergency: Wife Needed *Emily Forbes*	978 0 263 20301 1

HISTORICAL

Title	ISBN
The Virtuous Courtesan *Mary Brendan*	978 0 263 20198 7
The Homeless Heiress *Anne Herries*	978 0 263 20199 4
Rebel Lady, Convenient Wife *June Francis*	978 0 263 20200 7

MEDICAL™

Title	ISBN
Virgin Midwife, Playboy Doctor *Margaret McDonagh*	978 0 263 19894 2
The Rebel Doctor's Bride *Sarah Morgan*	978 0 263 19895 9
The Surgeon's Secret Baby Wish *Laura Iding*	978 0 263 19896 6
Italian Doctor, Full-time Father *Dianne Drake*	978 0 263 19897 3

Pure reading pleasure

MAY 2008 LARGE PRINT TITLES

ROMANCE

The Italian Billionaire's Ruthless Revenge *Jacqueline Baird*	978 0 263 20042 3
Accidentally Pregnant, Conveniently Wed *Sharon Kendrick*	978 0 263 20043 0
The Sheikh's Chosen Queen *Jane Porter*	978 0 263 20044 7
The Frenchman's Marriage Demand *Chantelle Shaw*	978 0 263 20045 4
Her Hand in Marriage *Jessica Steele*	978 0 263 20046 1
The Sheikh's Unsuitable Bride *Liz Fielding*	978 0 263 20047 8
The Bridesmaid's Best Man *Barbara Hannay*	978 0 263 20048 5
A Mother in a Million *Melissa James*	978 0 263 20049 2

HISTORICAL

The Vanishing Viscountess *Diane Gaston*	978 0 263 20154 3
A Wicked Liaison *Christine Merrill*	978 0 263 20155 0
Virgin Slave, Barbarian King *Louise Allen*	978 0 263 20156 7

MEDICAL™

The Magic of Christmas *Sarah Morgan*	978 0 263 19950 5
Their Lost-and-Found Family *Marion Lennox*	978 0 263 19951 2
Christmas Bride-To-Be *Alison Roberts*	978 0 263 19952 9
His Christmas Proposal *Lucy Clark*	978 0 263 19953 6
Baby: Found at Christmas *Laura Iding*	978 0 263 19954 3
The Doctor's Pregnancy Bombshell *Janice Lynn*	978 0 263 19955 0

0408 Gen Std LP

MILLS & BOON®
Pure reading pleasure

JUNE 2008 HARDBACK TITLES

ROMANCE

Hired: The Sheikh's Secretary Mistress	978 0 263 20302 8
Lucy Monroe	
The Billionaire's Blackmailed Bride	978 0 263 20303 5
Jacqueline Baird	
The Sicilian's Innocent Mistress	978 0 263 20304 2
Carole Mortimer	
The Sheikh's Defiant Bride *Sandra Marton*	978 0 263 20305 9
Italian Boss, Ruthless Revenge *Carol Marinelli*	978 0 263 20306 6
The Mediterranean Prince's Captive Virgin	
Robyn Donald	978 0 263 20307 3
Mistress: Hired for the Billionaire's Pleasure	978 0 263 20308 0
India Grey	
The Italian's Unwilling Wife *Kathryn Ross*	978 0 263 20309 7
Wanted: Royal Wife and Mother *Marion Lennox*	978 0 263 20310 3
The Boss's Unconventional Assistant	978 0 263 20311 0
Jennie Adams	
Inherited: Instant Family *Judy Christenberry*	978 0 263 20312 7
The Prince's Secret Bride *Raye Morgan*	978 0 263 20313 4
Milllionaire Dad, Nanny Needed! *Susan Meier*	978 0 263 20314 1
Falling for Mr Dark & Dangerous *Donna Alward*	978 0 263 20315 8
The Spanish Doctor's Love-Child *Kate Hardy*	978 0 263 20316 5
Her Very Special Boss *Anne Fraser*	978 0 263 20317 2

HISTORICAL

Miss Winthorpe's Elopement *Christine Merrill*	978 0 263 20201 4
The Rake's Unconventional Mistress	978 0 263 20202 1
Juliet Landon	
Rags-to-Riches Bride *Mary Nichols*	978 0 263 20203 8

MEDICAL™

Their Miracle Baby *Caroline Anderson*	978 0 263 19898 0
The Children's Doctor and the Single Mum	978 0 263 19899 7
Lilian Darcy	
Pregnant Nurse, New-Found Family	978 0 263 19900 0
Lynne Marshall	
The GP's Marriage Wish *Judy Campbell*	978 0 263 19901 7

MILLS & BOON®

Pure reading pleasure

0508 Gen Std LP

JUNE 2008 LARGE PRINT TITLES

ROMANCE

The Greek Tycoon's Defiant Bride 978 0 263 20050 8
Lynne Graham
The Italian's Rags-to-Riches Wife *Julia James* 978 0 263 20051 5
Taken by Her Greek Boss *Cathy Williams* 978 0 263 20052 2
Bedded for the Italian's Pleasure *Anne Mather* 978 0 263 20053 9
Cattle Rancher, Secret Son *Margaret Way* 978 0 263 20054 6
Rescued by the Sheikh *Barbara McMahon* 978 0 263 20055 3
Her One and Only Valentine *Trish Wylie* 978 0 263 20056 0
English Lord, Ordinary Lady *Fiona Harper* 978 0 263 20057 7

HISTORICAL

A Compromised Lady *Elizabeth Rolls* 978 0 263 20157 4
Runaway Miss *Mary Nichols* 978 0 263 20158 1
My Lady Innocent *Annie Burrows* 978 0 263 20159 8

MEDICAL™

Christmas Eve Baby *Caroline Anderson* 978 0 263 19956 7
Long-Lost Son: Brand New Family *Lilian Darcy* 978 0 263 19957 4
Their Little Christmas Miracle *Jennifer Taylor* 978 0 263 19958 1
Twins for a Christmas Bride *Josie Metcalfe* 978 0 263 19959 8
The Doctor's Very Special Christmas 978 0 263 19960 4
Kate Hardy
A Pregnant Nurse's Christmas Wish 978 0 263 19961 1
Meredith Webber